Irish Stories for Children

Irish Stories for Children

Selected and Introduced by
TOM MULLINS

MERCIER PRESS

Mercier Press
Douglas Village, Cork

Trade enquiries to CMD Distribution
55A Spruce Avenue, Stillorgan Industrial Park, Blackrock County Dublin

© Introduction Tom Mullins

Acknowledgement for permission to reprint the stories in this collection
can be found on page 111.

ISBN: 978 1 85635 027 3

A CIP record for this title is available from the British Library

Mercier Press receives financial assistance from
The Arts Council / An Chomairle Ealaíon

Printed by J. H. Haynes & Co. Ltd, Sparkford

CONTENTS

Introduction

Reading stories helps us all to see life in different ways. We can leave behind our ordinary everyday life and enter into other worlds; these can be in the past or in the future, can be real or imagined; we can have adventures with heroes and heroines, with ghosts and giants, with animals and monsters which leave us wishing and wondering. Stories introduce us to the rich variety of life.

The Irish tradition of story-telling is world-renowned. This country has kept alive for centuries its love of giving an exciting shape to life through story. There is such an enormous wealth within the Irish tradition of stories that sometimes young people are overcome by the amount and turn elsewhere for their reading pleasure. There is a loss in that; by not reading them one misses out on the special pleasure of seeing reflected in stories a distinctively Irish way of seeing the world. To read these stories is to discover an inheritance to treasure and savour for a lifetime.

This present selection is just a 'starter menu': It attempts to give a taste of the range and variety available within the Irish tradition. There are stories of all kinds, funny, sad, realistic, fanciful, ghostly and mysterious. Hopefully every one will find here some story to cherish so that they will be tempted to go forward into the great feast of Irish stories that awaits them from the past and the present.

The Giant's Wife

retold by
Felicity Hayes McCoy

Long ago there was a giant called Fionn McCool,
and Fionn McCool lived with his wife, Una, in a big
house in the County Tyrone. Across the sea in Scotland there lived another giant, and he lived in a
cave on the windy hillside and not in a house at all.

Now, Fionn McCool was a big giant. He was as
tall as a ten-storey house and as wide as the side of
a lorry. His head was the size of a cinema screen
and his little toe was as big as a doorstep. And he
could run a hundred miles without getting puffed.
Everyone in the neighbourhood used to boast
about how big he was, so his fame soon spread
through the four provinces of Ireland. And pretty
soon it spread across the sea to Scotland as well.

One morning, Una found Fionn sitting at the
kitchen table in front of his tub of porridge. He always had porridge for breakfast because there
weren't any cornflakes in those days. Even if there
had been, it would have taken twenty boxes to fill
Fionn.

He wasn't eating breakfast. He was just sitting
there gloomily, chewing his thumbs. Una was very
surprised.

'What's the matter with you,' she said. 'Is the
porridge lumpy?'

'No, it's grand,' said Fionn. 'But I've just had some news that's put me right off it.'

'What's that?' said Una.

Fionn asked her if she'd ever heard of the Scottish Giant.

'Of course I have,' said Una. 'I know all about him. He's a big, huge, fierce giant, even bigger than you are. And he's got wild, shaggy red hair and great, jagged, broken teeth and a big, knotted ash stick that's longer than a double-decker bus.'

'But what's he got to do with your breakfast?' she asked.

'He's coming to bash me up,' wailed Fionn. 'He says he's fed up of hearing about me.'

You see, the Scottish Giant had heard the people of Tyrone boasting about how big and strong Fionn was. So he'd decided to pay him a visit and see for himself.

'Well, that'll teach you not to go boasting about how big you are,' said Una.

'I don't,' said Fionn. 'Well, maybe I do a bit. But what am I going to do now?' he said. 'He'll be halfway here already.'

'Hold your whisht and have your breakfast,' said she. 'I'll think of something.'

And she did.

She left Fionn to light the fire and heat the oven, and off she went to the neighbour's house to borrow a griddle.

A griddle is a round, flat pan made of iron. People used them to bake bread over the fire.

Now, when Una had borrowed the biggest griddle she could find, she rushed back home to bake some bread. But when her loaf was shaped she pulled it in half and hid the griddle inside the dough. Then she baked it in the oven. So when it came out it had the hardest centre of any loaf ever made.

Then she made several other loaves as well, delicious, ordinary loaves that were crusty outside and soft within.

And then she sat down by the fire to do some sewing.

When she was finished, she held up a giant nightdress and a baby's cap that she'd made out of a tablecloth. Then she dressed Fionn up as a baby and tucked him up in a wicker basket by the fire.

Now Fionn had no idea what she was up to. But he did what she told him and he kept his mouth shut. As soon as he was in the basket, there was a knock on the door. And there was the Scottish Giant with his big stick.

Una smiled at him and she rocked the basket with her toe.

'Yes?' she said, 'were you looking for someone?'

And he told her he was looking for Fionn Mc-Cool.

'I'm afraid he's out at the moment,' said Una. 'He's just gone to knock down the town at the end of the valley.'

The Giant was impressed.

'Maybe you'd like to sit down and wait?' said Una. 'He'll only be ten minutes. Will you have a cup of tea in your hand?'

The Scottish Giant said he'd be delighted. But

he was a little worried because *he* didn't think he could flatten a whole town in ten minutes. And it seemed that Fionn could. So maybe it wasn't going to be that easy to bash him up after all.

Una got up to put the kettle on the fire. Then she shook her head sadly.

'Would you look at that,' she said. 'The wind's in the west again. Now if only Fionn were here he'd turn the house around. As it is, the fire will smoke and we'll have smoky tea.'

She sighed and she looked at the Scottish Giant. And what could he do but offer to help?

So up he got and off he went outside. And he shoved and he heaved and he hauled and he pushed until the house was turned right round.

By this time he was really worried. It was awfully hard turning that house. And Una had behaved as if Fionn did it easily. Meanwhile Fionn was shivering in his basket. You see, he'd never turned the house round in his life. He wouldn't have been strong enough.

As soon as the giant sat down again, Una gave him his tea.

'Here's a new-made loaf to go with it,' she said. And she handed him the loaf with the griddle in it.

He took a big bite. Then his tooth hit the griddle with an awful crack and he let a roar out of him that shook the house from attic to cellar.

'What's the matter?' said Una.

'Glory be to God, ma'am,' said the Scottish Giant, 'that bread's like iron.'

'Nonsense,' said Una. 'I only made it this morning. Sure the baby could eat that and come to no harm.'

She turned away and crossed to the basket by the fire. Then she picked up one of the ordinary loaves and handed it to Fionn. And Fionn ate the loaf in two bites.

The Scottish Giant couldn't believe his eyes. He rushed over to the basket and then jumped back in alarm.

'That's a grand big baby, ma'am,' he said nervously. 'What age is he?'

Una shook her head.

'Oh it's nice of you to say so,' she said, 'but he's not big at all for six months. Sure, his Daddy's ashamed of the size he is.'

'And is that a bit of the Daddy's bread he's after chewing?' said the Giant.

'It is,' said Una. 'He's got a grand set of teeth in his head, thank God. Fionn had all his teeth at two weeks, of course, but this lad's not doing badly. Would you like to feel them?' And she took his hand and guided it into Fionn's mouth.

Well Fionn mightn't have been as clever as his wife but he wasn't a fool altogether. He knew what to do when he felt the Scottish Giant's hand between his teeth. He bit him. He bit him as hard and as long as he could. And he didn't stop till the Giant was howling for mercy.

Una let on to be horrified.

'Oh, God forgive you, you bold child,' she said. 'Is it biting the nice gentleman and he only trying to be friendly? Just wait till your Daddy gets home.'

But if that was the baby, the Scottish Giant

wasn't waiting to see the Daddy. He was out of the house and away down the road before Una had finished speaking. And he didn't stop running till he was back in his own cave on the windy hillside in the north of Scotland.

Cliona's Wave

Sinéad de Valera

Loud music, as from the surging of a wave, is occasionally heard in the harbour of Glandore, County Cork, both in calm and stormy weather. It is the forerunner of the shifting of the wind to the northwest. It is called the 'Tonn Cliona' or Cliona's Wave and was supposed to portend the death of some great personage.

King Turlough and his Queen Sive had their palace near Glandore, in County Cork. They were married many years and had no children. At last a beautiful baby girl was born. She was called Ethna and was the joy and pride of her parent's hearts.

One lovely day the king and queen were seated at a window in the palace, looking at the beautiful scene that lay before them.

> Cloudless sky and sparkling sea,
> Cliff and shore and forest tree,
> Glen and stream and mountain blue,
> Burst at once upon the view.

'Who would not be happy,' said Turlough, 'while looking on such a scene?'

'Well, you and I are certainly very happy,' the queen replied, 'and it is a joy to think that little Ethna is heiress to all this beauty. There she is,

sleeping peacefully in her cradle under the hawthorn tree, with her faithful nurse by her side.'

'Sometimes,' said the king, 'I wonder if the
nurse is so faithful. It has been whispered to me
that she cares more about Fergus, the gardener,
than she does about our little Ethna.'

'Oh, don't mind those idle rumours,' the queen
said. 'I am sure she is very attentive to the child.
Let us walk down to the sea. It is a pity to be in-
doors on such a day.'

'Look how calm the water is,' said the king. 'It
is almost without a ripple, except where the wave-
lets break on the beach.'

'Yes, but there is a swell on the sea and the
wind is turning to the north-east.'

Suddenly, a loud noise was heard, a noise as
from the surging of a wave. Both Turlough and
Sive trembled and turned pale.

'That is Cliona's wave!' cried the king in great
alarm.

'Yes,' said the queen, 'the wave that gives warn-
ing that some terrible sorrow is to come to us. Can
we do nothing to lessen the fairy's power?'

'Alas, no! No one is strong enough to lessen the
power of the fairy, Cliona.'

They returned in haste to the palace. Everything there showed signs of trouble and confusion.

'Oh, what has happened?' cried the queen.

There was silence for a moment and then Turlough and Sive were told that their dear child was
lost. The nurse had left the baby sleeping under the
hawthorn tree and had gone some distance away to
speak to the gardener. When she returned the child

was gone. She had been stolen by the fairies.

'I knew,' said Turlough, 'that some great sorrow was coming to us when we heard the sound of Cliona's Wave.'

'Oh, why,' asked Sive, turning to the nurse, 'did you leave our child alone?'

'It is just as if she had died,' said the king, 'for we shall never see her again.'

From that time happiness and peace were gone from the palace. Sorrow and gloom reigned in their stead. Years went by without bringing any tidings of Ethna. Turlough and Sive tried to rule wisely and look after the welfare of their subjects, but they never ceased to pine for the child they had lost.

One day Sive was walking along a road just outside the palace when she saw a woman and a little boy coming towards her. As the woman drew nearer, the queen saw that she looked very tired and ill. In a moment she had fallen to the ground. One of the queen's waiting women hurried into the palace to call for help. When the woman was brought in, it was found that she was dying. She whispered to the queen: 'My husband, who was a chieftain in a territory some miles east from here, was killed when defending his home from his enemies. I travelled here to ask you to befriend my little Donal when I am gone.'

In a few moments the woman was dead.

The queen felt it was her duty to take care of the little boy. Gradually she came to love him as if he were her own child. She and the king determined to make him their heir. They often spoke to him of Ethna and it became the great wish of his heart to bring her back to her home.

Years passed and Donal grew to be a fine, handsome youth. He was as good as he was handsome. He had a great love of the sea and used to go for many miles from land in a boat which the queen had given him. Sometimes he would take provisions with him and would spend hours on the water.

One warm August day when the sea was like a beautiful spreading lake under a blue sky, Donal ventured farther and farther from the shore. As he went southward, he saw in the distance a small island. It seemed to be covered with emeralds and rubies. As he drew nearer, he saw that rows of rowan trees grew round the coast. Their foliage and berries were what he had thought were gems glistening in the sunshine.

A little cove faced him as he approached the island. He made fast his boat and went in on the island. From the trees came the sound of human voices and, to his amazement, he found that these voices belonged to birds perched on the trees. Numbers of birds were there, brown, black, green and other colours, all chattering away in human speech.

While Donal was wondering at what he saw and heard, he noticed a strange-looking house in the centre of the island. It was built of stone and had a long, sloping roof.

The birds continued to talk. Donal lay down on the sward near the house and listened to them.

'Yesterday,' said the pigeon, 'I flew to Glandore Castle and rested in the hawthorn tree in the garden. The king and queen were sitting under the tree. They were speaking sadly of Princess Ethna who was carried away to fairyland many years ago.'

'They will never see the same Ethna again,' said the raven in a harsh, croaking voice. 'The fairy Cliona holds her a captive in her court.'

'Oh, you always have the worst news!' exclaimed the thrush.

'Well, I know what I am talking about,' retorted the raven.

'Peace, peace,' said the gentle voice of the dove.

'Yes,' said the little wren, 'let us be bright and cheerful.'

'Was Ethna the name of the princess?' asked the swallow from her nest under the roof of the house.

'Yes,' replied the pigeon, 'Ethna was her name.'

'Well, then I know where she is. In the spring, when we swallows were coming back to Ireland, we flew over a fairy fort some miles north of Glandore. I stopped to take a sip of water from a river near by. I saw a mortal maiden in the fort and heard the fairies call her Ethna.'

Just then Donal saw a boat approaching the island. An old, bent man came on shore.

'You are the first visitor that has come to my island home,' he said to Donal, 'and I bid you welcome.'

Donal thanked him and told him he had been much interested in listening to the conversation of the birds.

'Yes,' said the old man, 'these birds see and hear a great deal in their flights from the island

and, as they have the gift of speech, they tell me everything that happens.'

'I have heard very important news from them,' said Donal.

'What is that news?'

'It is about the Princess Ethna, who was years ago taken from her father's home by the fairies. The birds say she is in Cliona's fort.'

The old man shook his head.

'Cliona has wonderful magic powers and, even if you could reach the fort, it would be difficult to reach the princess. I can help you, however, if you are brave enough to attempt to bring Ethna back.'

'I would do anything to restore her to her parents.'

'Well, then I will give all the help I can but there will be difficulties and hardships in your way. Cliona's fort is several miles north from Glandore. I will send the pigeon to be your guide by day and the owl to lead you by night.'

'But how will I know the place?' asked Donal.

'You will come to a great rock in the middle of a circular space. Round this rock is a row of smaller stones. This place is Carrig Cliona, that is Cliona's rock. It is useless to approach the fort by day. Wait for a moonlight night!'

'The moon is full at present and I would like to reach the fort tomorrow night.'

'You can do that if you return home now and set out in the morning.'

'I will take the fastest horse in the stable,' said Donal.

'No,' said the man, 'You must go on foot. When

you have travelled about twenty miles, you will come to a little house half-hidden by trees. I will send one of my birds to tell the woman of the house to expect you.'

'But how shall I succeed in freeing Ethna from the fairy's spell?'

'That will not be easy. Cliona is very clever. She can take the form of different animals. She can become a deer, a hound or a rabbit but whatever shape she assumes, her green eyes remain the same. Before you set out on your journey tomorrow, cut a branch of the hawthorn tree in the palace garden, a branch with berries on it. If you can manage to strike Cliona with the branch, you will have her in your power and she must do as you wish.'

'And how shall I find Ethna?'

'Command Cliona to call her forth and the princess will gladly come. Do not on any account enter the fort yourself. You must not eat, drink nor speak from the time you leave the island till you reach the house among the trees. Now take my blessing and hasten away.'

As Donal sailed from the shore, the birds sang in a chorus:

> *Happy will the princess be,*
> *When young Donal sets her free,*
> *He will break the cruel spell,*
> *And the fairy's power will quell.*
> *May kind fortune on him smile,*
> *As he leaves our wooded isle.*

Everyone had retired to rest before Donal returned. The night was warm and he slept in a summer house in the garden. Early in the morning he went to the hawthorn tree to cut the berried branch. There, sitting on the top of the tree was the pigeon which was to be his guide.

As Donal travelled on, the day became very hot and he felt tired, hungry and thirsty. He saw a woman coming toward him. She had a basket full of delicious fruit in one hand and a glass of mead in the other. She offered him the fruit and the mead. Donal longed to take them but he could not speak, eat nor drink. He gave one longing look at the good things, shook his head and passed on.

When he had gone a little distance he looked back to the place where he had met the woman but she was nowhere to be seen, though that part of the road was quite straight, without bend or turning. The pigeon acted as his guide till he reached the house among the trees. Then the bird turned and flew southward. To his great surprise, he saw, standing at the door of the house, the woman who had offered him the food and drink.

'You are heartily welcome,' she said.

Donal thanked her and followed her into the house.

'You have bravely borne hunger, thirst and weariness,' said the woman, 'and now you will have your reward.'

She led Donal into the room where a delicious meal was prepared for him. When he had finished his meal she told him to go into the inner room.

'There is a bed,' she said, 'where you can rest

until you hear the owl's cry.'

Donal was glad to rest and soon he fell into a deep sleep. He was awakened by the hooting of the owl. He went to the window and by the light of the moon saw the bird on the branch of a tree. As he was leaving the house, the woman said to him:

'If you succeed in your effort to free the princess, there will be food and rest for both of you here on your return journey. Take this horn,' she said, 'and blow three times when you reach the fairy fort. Cliona will then appear before you.'

Donal again thanked the woman and followed in the direction in which the owl flitted from tree to tree. He came in sight of Cliona's rock. He blew the horn once, twice, three times. Out from the fort walked Cliona. She was very beautiful but there was a cruel gleam in her green eyes.

As she came near to where Donal stood, he attempted to strike her with the hawthorn branch. Immediately, she changed into a white rabbit and ran round and round the court. The darkness fell. Donal felt something descend upon his shoulder. It was the owl whose voice whispered in his ear:

'I will tell you when the rabbit is coming close to where you stand and will warn you when to strike ...'

'Now,' said the owl after a few seconds.

A piercing shriek was heard. The darkness cleared away and Cliona stood there, weeping and wringing her hands.

'Command the princess Ethna to come forth,' said Donal.

'Come, Ethna, come,' called Cliona, as she herself disappeared into the fort.

From the centre of the fort Ethna approached the surrounding rocks. She stepped outside and looked around her in wonder and joy.

'Oh!' she exclaimed, 'what a beautiful world! But where shall I find the loving friends I have so often seen in my dreams?'

'Come with me,' said Donal, 'and their joy will be even greater than yours when you are all re-united.'

The owl led them back to the little house where the woman gave them a warm welcome. When they were departing on their homeward journey she said to them:

'There will be great rejoicing in the palace when you return and soon there will be a happy wedding there.'

The king and queen wept for joy when they saw their loved child again. Everyone in the palace shared in their delight.

The woman's words came true, for Donal and Ethna were married and lived happily ever after.

The Four Magpies

Sigerson Clifford

When the big foxy cat saw the donkey and cart outside the door and old Tim reddening his pipe for the road he knew his master was going to the village and he'd be alone until nightfall. When the mood took himself he slipped away from the house for the length of a week without as much as by-your-leave but he kicked up an almighty fuss whenever Tim left him alone for even half a day.

After the fashion of people who live by themselves in lonely places Tim always talked to his cat as if he was human.

'I'll be back before dark, I tell you, and I'll buy a few mackerel for you from Seamuseen O. Will that satisfy you, now?'

The cat steered the schooner-mast of his tail between Tim's legs and miaowed fiercely.

"Tisn't that you deserve mackerel, you lazy scoundrel. The house ate with mice and you're doing nothing about it. I declare to Jericho if the mice formed a pipers' band you'd march at the head of it carrying the banner instead of gobbling them up, whatever seed or breed of cats you're sprung from, you scamp.'

The cat followed Tim to where the boreen melted into the grandeur of the main road, and perched

25

on the fence looking after him and crying as though he smelt the end of the world coming across the mountain. He stood there wailing until the cart rattled around a bend in the road and then curled up under a furze bush and fell asleep.

Beyond the Three Eye Bridge, Tim heard a chuckle in the air and looked up. It was a magpie making a movable black and white patch on the tent of the sky.

'One for luck,' said Tim. 'That's a good start to the day anyhow.'

A second magpie leaped up from the field behind the river and climbed to meet the first.

'Two for joy,' said old Tim, 'That's better again, faith.'

Half a mile further on in the Dean's field he saw a third magpie perched on a cow's back like a cheeky jockey.

'Three to get married,' quoted Tim. 'What do you think of that for advice, Barney?'

The donkey threw up his head meaning to say they were better off as they were with no woman flinging orders about like oats to goslings.

'Begor,' said Tim, 'there's no sense in tackling at seventy-five what you were afraid of at twenty-one. Three to get married, fine girl you are!'

The words of an old ballad, about a damsel who lived on the mountains and whose stockings were white, ran into his mind and he began to sing them softly to shorten the journey. At the outskirts of the village he saw Razor Sullivan's small son, Daneen, standing beside the gate.

'Hello Tim,' the boy said, 'I'll give you three

guesses as to what I have behind my back.'

Tim halted the donkey, pursed his lips, and wrinkled his forehead to add importance to the occasion.

'Is it Finn MacCool's magic razor that was sharp enough to shave a mouse asleep?'

'No, no,' cried Daneen with delight. 'Guess again, Tim.'

'Is it the eye of the King of the Fomoricans that could see around corners?'

'You're miles out, Tim. Guess again.'

'Then it must be the golden angel that flew off with the Rock of Cashel last week.'

The boy whooped with delight at his victory, and showed him the young magpie he had hidden behind his back.

'I found him in the wood and I'm going to make a pet of him and, maybe, teach him to talk,' said the boy.

The magpie said nothing but eyed Tim as though he was measuring him for a coffin.

The old man drove into the village, the jingle about the magpies nagging at his brain. Four to die, the last line ran of it. He felt as healthy as a herring, but then it wasn't the sick ones who went all the time. Patch Fitzmaurice saw four magpies before he died a year ago and he was never a day sick in his life.

By the time he drew level with the chapel he decided to make his will without further delay. The village was too small to support a solicitor but Patrick Monaghan who kept the hardware shop would oblige him. He tied the donkey to the pole outside the window, went in and whispered his business to Monaghan who sat him in the parlour while he fetched pen and paper.

'I'll have to make my mark, Mr Monaghan, for I can't read or write. My father, God rest him, didn't trouble to make a scholar out of me,' said Tim.

Mr Monaghan smiled under his foxy moustache and filled his fountain pen.

'Education can have its drawbacks, too, Tim,' he replied. He didn't say what the drawbacks were.

The will was a simple matter. Tim had £500 in the post office, one acre of land, a house and a cat. With the exception of £20 for Masses he left everything to his favourite niece, Abigail Falvey, on condition that she looked after his cat. The will was witnessed by Monaghan's two servant-girls. Tim gave him a pound for his trouble and went out to his donkey.

Further up the street he ran into his neighbour, James Donnelly. James had a scowl on his face that stretched from the peak of his cap to the knot of his tie.

'What's worrying you now, James?' he asked.

'It's my Aunt Mary's will,' replied Donnelly. 'There's going to be law over it and by the time we're through with the courts there won't be a shilling in the kitty. That eegit, Monaghan, made a mess of the will when he was drawing it up.'

'Did he, faith!' said Tim, trying to look unconcerned.

When James was gone he sat in the cart thinking about his own will and wondering what he should do. He saw Father O'Carroll going in the chapel gate and he hurried after him. He took the will from his pocket and handed it to him.

'It's my will, Father. I'd be deeply obliged if you'd take a look at it and see if 'tis in order. You see, I can't read or write.'

Father O'Carroll read the will.

'Yes, it seems to be quite in order. You've left everything to your niece, Abigail Falvey, with the exception of £20 for Masses and £50 to your good friend, Patrick Monaghan.'

Tim thanked him and took back the will. As he walked towards the street he tore it into little pieces and made a ball of it in the heel of his fist. He returned to Monaghan's shop and went in the door. Monaghan came to serve him with a £50 smile under his moustache.

'I've run short of money,' Tim explained, 'and I was wondering if you could lend me a pound until the next time I'm in the village. '

'Certainly, Tim, and ten of them,' said Monaghan.

'One will do,' Tim told him. 'I hate owing too much money.'

He went out the door and didn't bother to look back.

The Ant

Michael Scott

An Ant doesn't look like very much, and it is so small you might even walk on it without noticing. But the next time you are out walking, be careful, and watch where you walk, and try not to step on any of the tiny creatures. You never know when an ant might be able to help you.

This is a story about the time a poor farmer in the west of Ireland helped an ant ...

Martin Newman put his hands on his hips, turned and looked back across the fields. Although he had been working since sunrise, and it was now well into the afternoon, he was only half finished. The field was full of long raised lines of earth, and each line had thick green plants growing up out of them. They were potatoes. On one side of the field, the plants lay on their sides and pale golden-brown potatoes lay in neat piles on the earth.

Martin rubbed his hands together, brushing off the heavy clay and tried to guess how long it would take him to finish the potato picking. He was a tall, thin young man, with thin black hair and dark sunburnt skin. His eyes were the same colour as the sky – pale blue. And now his eyes were squinting against the glare of the sun as he glanced up into the heavens. He guessed that it was about three or four o'clock in the afternoon, and then he looked back at the field again. He didn't think he was going to get finished today – but tomorrow was market day, and the first potatoes of the season would fetch the highest prices.

The young man sighed and shook his head. He would have a quick lunch and then start again. He lifted a plastic bag off the stone wall where he had left it in his coat, and pulled out the sandwiches his wife had made for him earlier that morning. In the bottom of the bag he found that she had also slipped in an apple. Martin perched on the rough stone wall and began to eat his late lunch.

As he was eating he saw storm clouds gathering in the distance, out over the sea. Old Paddy Forrest his neighbour, had told him that there would be a storm that day, and Old Paddy was never wrong about the weather.

Martin bit into his apple with a crunch and looked over his field again. He did some working out in his head and guessed that he would have the field finished by midday tomorrow. But that would be too late – the market started early in the morning. And if it rained now, the clay would get heavy and sticky, and make his work all the more difficult. He finished the apple and dropped the core by his feet, although he carefully bundled up the plastic his sandwiches had been wrapped in and put it back into his bag. Martin knew the apple would rot back into the ground, but the plastic would not.

'Back to work,' he sighed and trudged across the field to continue pulling up the potato plants and shaking the potatoes free from the roots.

Martin Newman worked as hard as he could for the rest of the afternoon. He would stop every now and again and straighten up and look back over his shoulder at the storm clouds which were much nearer now. Soon the sun was swallowed up behind them, and a cold wind blew across the field, making the young man shiver. The storm rolled in quickly – far more quickly than he had thought it would – and he only had a few more rows to pick when it began to rain.

A single drop fell first, splattering onto the green plant in his hand, little drops of silver water shooting off in all directions. Then another drop struck his face, running ice-cold down his cheek. Another drop hit him on the back of the neck and trickled down the collar of his shirt. And then it looked as if someone had turned on a tap – water came down in a solid sheet. Martin turned up the collar of his shirt and ran for cover.

He reached the stone wall and jumped straight over it, and then he huddled down on the far side. Because the wind was blowing in from the sea, the rain was also falling in that direction and he was quite dry where he was in the shadow of the wall. He remembered his bag and coat then which were still up on the wall and he reached up with one hand to pull them down. His coat was already soaking wet, but he draped it over his shoulders, brought his knees up to his chest and folded his arms around them. He would head for home when the rain eased off a little.

There was nothing for him to do, so the young man leaned against the wall, feeling the cold stones poke into his back, and watched the rain fall. He watched it hit the hard earth and bounce, until it looked as if there was a fine haze lying a few inches off the ground. And then a little stream of water wriggled its way out from under the stones of the wall, and twisted and curled its way past his feet. The water was coming from his field, and soon began to carry along small leaves and twigs. However, as the rain grew heavier and heavier, larger pieces of wood and small clumps of earth wound their way past Martin's boots.

And then something white was carried down on the water. It was the apple core that Martin had dropped on the ground – and perched on the back of the apple was a small black ant. The apple tumbled over and stuck, and the ant was caught under the little stream of water. Martin saw its long feelers waving about and its legs struggling to reach the surface. But just as it managed to climb up onto the top of the apple again, a twig swept down and knocked the little creature off into the water.

Without thinking Martin reached down and scooped the little ant up in the palm of his hand. He brought his head close to his hand to look at the ant and then gently blew on it drying it off. Soon its feelers, which had become stuck to its body, were waving in the air again, and it walked across Martin's hand and seemed to stare him straight in the eye.

'There you are now, little fellow,' Martin said.

'That will teach you to go out when it's raining. But what are we going to do with you, eh?' he asked. He looked around for some place to put the ant. 'I'll leave you here,' he decided, 'you should be safe enough.'

Martin brought his hand close to the stone wall, and gently eased the little ant off his palm with his finger. The small creature scuttled up onto the wall and disappeared into a crack in the stones. The young man glanced up into the sky – but it was still dark with heavy grey storm clouds, and the rain showed no sign of easing up. 'I suppose I had better head for home,' he said to himself. He sighed deeply. 'I'm never going to get those potatoes picked in time for market.' And then, pulling his coat up over his head, Martin set off at a run for home.

The rain eventually stopped close to midnight and then the clouds rolled quickly away, leaving a full moon shining pale and silver in the sky. The stars were like sharp little points of light, and, away in the distance, a single star fell slowly to earth, leaving a long ghostly trail behind it.

Martin Newman's fields were deserted, and the only noise was the trickling, dripping sound of water, as it fell from leaves and bushes and soaked into the ground.

And then something moved in the centre of the field.

It looked like a shadow. A broad, flat shadow – almost like a blanket thrown on the earth. But this blanket was moving. It swept out across the field and gathered around the first of the potato plants and then there was the sound of crunching and scraping, and slowly the bush toppled over, exposing the pale potatoes beneath. Part of the shadow moved onto the next bush, and soon it fell in a shower of earth. And then something even stranger happened. Parts of this dark shadow broke up and gathered around each potato – and the potato rose up a fraction of an inch above the ground and began to glide along! Little piles of potatoes began to form about the field, and by the time the sun came up and Martin Newman's footsteps rang along the track that led to his field, every potato plant had been dug up and all the potatoes were arranged in neat little bundles, ready to put into bags.

Martin stood by the wall, with his mouth open in astonishment. What had happened? A hundred thoughts ran through his mind. Had the fairies helped him, or was it perhaps ghosts, or had he done all the work yesterday and just forgotten about it?

The young man shook his head. He didn't know – and he didn't think he would ever know.

'Thank you,' he shouted aloud, 'whoever, whatever you are. Thank you.' So, whistling happily to himself, he hopped over the wall and began to gather up the potatoes into thick bags.

In the next field a dark black shadow stopped when it heard the voice. Then it moved on and began to break up and it streamed into a deep hole beneath the wall, and quickly disappeared.

But if you had looked very closely at the shadow, you would have seen that it was made up out of millions of tiny black ants.

The Fox and the Hedgehog

Michael Scott

Everyone knows the story about the tortoise and the hare, but very few people know that Irish storytellers were telling a very similar story many hundreds of years ago ...

Sionnach the fox looked up suddenly, his pointed ears twitching, his wet black nose wrinkling. Something was coming. He lay flat on the ground and his brown coat so matched the piles of golden fallen leaves that it was impossible to see him. His nose wrinkled again, testing the damp forest air, sorting out the different forest smells: the wet ground, the rotting leaves and the sap of the different trees. He recognised the smell of the birds and the insects, faint and in the distance, he caught the hated smell of smoke, the sign of man. But it was the final and different odour that he couldn't make out. It was a musty, musky, dry sort of smell, and yet it also smelt damp and earthy.

Something rattled through some dry leaves and Sionnach froze. He felt his heart beginning to beat and he had the sudden urge to sneeze – but that always happened at times like this. More leaves rustled and then what looked like a small walking

36

ball of leaves stopped right in front of the fox's hiding place. For a moment Sionnach didn't know what it was, but then he suddenly recognised it – it was a hedgehog.

Dinner, Sionnach thought, and he leaped out in front of the hedgehog.

Grainne squealed with fright, and then she rolled herself up into a spiny ball. What a stupid fox, she thought.

Sionnach looked at the ball of spines in front of him and had second thoughts. Perhaps it had not been such a good idea just to jump out in front of the hedgehog like this. But he decided to do the best he could. 'Well, I have you now,' he said, grinning.

'Have you?' Grainne asked, her voice sounding muffled because her head was tucked down and into her body.

Sionnach padded around the ball and tapped it with his paw. *Ouch!* Those spines hurt! What was he going to do with the hedgehog?

'What are you going to do with me?' Grainne asked, almost as if she could read his mind.

'Well, I'm going to eat you of course,' Sionnach said.

'How?' she asked.

But Sionnach didn't answer, because he wasn't too sure himself.

After a while, Grainne said, 'Why don't you let me go – I'm sure there will be something tastier along in a little while.'

But Sionnach stubbornly shook his head. 'No, I'm not going to let you go. I'm going to eat you.'

37

'You will hurt yourself,' Grainne said, with what sounded like a sigh.

The fox looked at the spines and thought again. He had once run into a thorn bush when he was being chased by a pack of dogs, and he still remembered how sharp those thorns had been. Eating the hedgehog would be like chewing a thorn bush.

'Why can't you let me go?' Grainne asked.

Sionnach shook his head again. 'What would happen if the other foxes heard about it?' he asked. 'They would only laugh at me, and say I couldn't even eat a simple hedgehog. I have my reputation to think of,' he added proudly.

'A lot of foxes won't eat hedgehogs,' she said after a while, 'not unless they're very hungry. Are you very hungry?'

'Well not very. But I wouldn't mind some dinner now.'

'Well, I'm terribly sorry, but I am not on the menu for today. Now I can lie here all day, and all night too, but you'll have to leave. So, you're just wasting your time.'

Sionnach sat back on his haunches and looked at the spiky ball in front of him. If he turned her over he might be able to ... but no, he shook his head. To do that would mean either using his paws, or his nose, and he didn't want to get either of those spiked. So, what he would have to do would be to trick the lady hedgehog. He closed his eyes and wondered just what he would do.

Time passed, and the sun moved slowly across the heavens, sending slanting beams through the branches. The autumn leaves turned bright red and gold, orange and bronze in the light, and it gave everything a rich, warm glow. Two of the last butterflies of summer chased each other through the trees, the sun turning their red and black wings to brilliant spots of colour. They twisted around, darting and turning, resting for a few seconds on the warm branches of the trees before darting off again.

Sionnach watched them, their beautiful shapes and colours distracting him from the still curled-up hedgehog on the ground before his two front paws. And then he had an idea. He gave a short, sharp bark with excitement.

'I've had an idea,' he said.

There was no movement or sound from the hedgehog – well almost no sound. The fox's sharp ears caught a low buzzing sort of sound, and it seemed to be coming from the hedgehog. He turned his head and brought his sharp ears down close to the small bundle ... and found that it was snoring!

'Wake up,' he barked.

'I'm awake, I'm awake,' Grainne grumbled. 'What's wrong with you now?'

'I've had an idea,' Sionnach said.

'So?'

'I'm going to let you go,' the fox said quickly.

'Well I don't believe you,' Grainne said, just as quickly. 'It's a trick or a trap.'

'Why would I do that ?' Sionnach asked in his most innocent voice.

'Because you're hungry and you want to eat me,' the hedgehog said.

'Well ... ' the fox began.

'Well what?' Grainne demanded.

'Well, I'm going to let you go. I am going to count up to one hundred and then I'm going to come after you. If I catch you, then I'll eat you; but if you reach the river before I catch you then I'll let you go.'

'How do I know I can trust you?' Grainne asked.

Sionnach looked hurt. 'Because I'm a fox, and while we may be tricky and maybe we sometimes don't tell the full truth, we never tell lies.'

'So, if I can reach the river, then I'm safe?' Grainne asked.

Sionnach nodded. 'That's right.'

'And you'll count to a hundred first – all the way to a hundred?'

'All the way,' he promised.

'When do we start?' she asked.

'As soon as you wish,' he said.

Suddenly the hedgehog was up and running – well, waddling really – as quickly as she could into the forest. She was so quick that the fox was not quite ready, and she was already disappearing along a winding track before he started counting.

'One ... two ... three ... four. One ... two ... three ... four.'

Foxes can only count to four – one for each paw. So Sionnach did a quick sum and divided four into one hundred and came up with twenty-five. He began to scratch little marks in the ground with his nails for every 'one, two, three, four'. When he had twenty-five scratches he would go after the hedgehog.

Meanwhile, Grainne had no sooner lost sight of the fox when she stopped and crept into the thickest thorn bush she could find and quickly wormed her way into its very centre. She knew that she could not outrun the quicker fox, and she knew that he would be able to follow her scent there, but what she was hoping was that he would not be able to get in, and would eventually get tired and go away. Once she was in the very heart of the bush, she gave a huge sigh of relief.

'Is something the matter?' a thin, high voice asked above her head.

Grainne looked up to find a sparrow peering down through the branches.

'A fox is after me,' Grainne said, and quickly told the sparrow what had happened. 'Oh, I know that fox,' said the sparrow – whose name was Gealbhan – said, 'and once he finds out you're in here, he will sit outside for days and days. He doesn't give up easily.'

'But I've got to get home to my little ones,' Grainne said, 'I can't sit here for days. What am I going to do?'

Gealbhan cocked his small head to one side for a few minutes and then said, 'Do you know of any other hedgehog living near the river?'

'Well there is my sister, Grainneog,' Grainne said. 'She lives in a tree stump right on the river bank. That was where I was going when the fox stopped me.'

'Well then,' Gealbhan said, 'here's what we'll do then ...'

'ONE, TWO, THREE, four. One two, three, four.' Sionnach took a deep breath and said as quickly as he could, 'One, two, three, four. Here I come!'

The fox dashed down along the path, his long, low body weaving through the trees and bushes, his bushy tail flowing out behind him. At first he could catch faint traces of hedgehog scent, but after a while all traces of it disappeared. He began to get a little worried when there was neither sight nor smell of the creature, but he soon began to pick up the damp smell of the river, and he decided he would go there before turning back to check and see if she had decided to hide along the track. He was quite sure he was going to catch her, because of course, there was no way such a small, slow creature could outrun him, Sionnach the fox.

The fox ran out of the bushes and skidded to a halt in the soft ground of the river bank. He stopped – right in front of a hedgehog. 'What took you so long?' she asked, and curled up in a tight ball.

Sionnach looked at her in amazement for long moments before silently trotting away, shaking his head. He never did work out just how the hedgehog had beaten him to the river bank, and he never tried to eat a hedgehog again.

Of course, all that happened was that Gealbhan the sparrow had flown to Grainneog, Grainne's sister, and told her what had happened, and she met the fox when he arrived. Foxes might be very clever, but they can be very stupid sometimes too.

The Trapper

Sigerson Clifford

When Cobbler Carthy's pipe was smoked to ashes, he arose and flicked his eyes over the birds swinging from the rafters in our house, the two goldfinches by the back door and the red-breasted linnet beside the dresser.

'Which is the best, Tom?' he asked my father. My father pointed at the nearest goldfinch.

'Dick there is the champion. The best bird I have handled. He'd crack the rafters for you. I wouldn't swap that fellow for a fifty acre farm.'

'He must be good so,' agreed the cobbler. He took the cover from his pipe and knocked the ashes carefully into the fire as he saw my mother's eye trained on him.

'I suppose,' he continued, 'you've noticed the wife's niece staying with us for the past week.'

'I have,' said my father. 'A fine healthy girl she is God bless her.'

'Well,' said the cobbler, coming to the point at last, 'the Glenbay Trapper sent a challenge by her. He'll meet you Sunday week, weather permitting, in Rearden's field by the river. The first man to trap a goldfinch wins and the winner gets his opponent's call-bird for a prize. Are you agreeable?'

My father, who was the best bird trapper in our

43

parish, nodded. 'I'm agreeable. I haven't any bird-lime at the moment, but I can make some to-morrow. Sunday week, you said? Tell the Glenbay Trapper I'll be there.'

The cobbler moved towards the half-door.

"Twill be a good contest and this parish will have a stocking of money on you. The girl is going home this evening and I'll send your message by her. Good luck now, whatever.'

On the day of the contest, I was the proudest lad since Lucifer and I left the house with Dick, the call-bird, swinging by my side, and my father on my left hand with his head held high as befitting a champion on his way to uphold the honour of his parish. At the bottom of the Rocky Road the bird-men, fully a score of them, were waiting on us. We all marched two by two like Dooley's army to the river.

When we arrived we found the Glenbay Trapper and his supporters sprawled on the grass by the river's edge. He nodded at Dick in his green cage.

'That's a good finch you have there, Tom,' he told my father.

'Mhuise,' deprecated my father, 'he's only mid-dling.'

As he had a Glenbay wife and, in consequence, a leg in each parish, Cobbler Carty was elected judge. He called the contestants to him and ex-plained the rules.

He tossed a penny for choice of position in the field and my father won. As we walked away from the men the cobbler shouted, 'Lay your bets now, lads,' and we could hear the snapping of catches as the careful country purses opened and shut. Rearden's field, which grew most of the parish's crop of thistles, was a favourite feeding-ground of the goldfinches.

My father who had spent many hours bird-watching from the bushes that rimmed it, walked straight to the eastern corner and stood the cage among the purple thistles. Then he spat on his fingers and limed the sprig he had brought with him. We went back to the bushes and waited.

It was agony hiding there in the leaves, listening to the airy chatter of the men and the placid drone of the river, and peering about the sky for the expected birds. I looked at my father. He was quite silent, his face white and tense as he stared steadfastly at the east.

A nerve in his neck throbbed against the skin as though there were a little spring bubbling somewhere in his throat. His long thin fingers fidgeted like aspen leaves. It was the first time I saw him really nervous.

Below us the Glenbay Trapper suddenly whistled and pointed to the south-east. We looked and saw the charm of goldfinches high in the sky and as they came nearer we could hear the tinkle of their twittering like silver coins tossed among stones. Bigger and louder they grew until they were flying above the field.

'They won't land,' said someone in a fierce whisper. 'Bad luck to them, they suspect something.'

Then Dick, our call-bird, began to sing. Music

gushed from his small pulsing throat, louder and louder until the field and sky throbbed with it. Bright-eyed I listened and fancied I could see the notes surging upwards in a silver wave to drench the goldfinches flying overhead.

'God!' cried the cobbler excitedly, 'that's what I call a song bird. Whist! Whist! He's bringing them down.'

And he was. Suddenly the charm stopped dead and swished to earth like a fistful of flung gravel. They crowded the thistles about Dick's cage, peering at him with their crimson heads cocked sideways and fluttering their dainty yellow wings.

Breathlessly we watched them, every man jack of us stiff as stone statues behind the screen of bushes. Then a voice husky with excitement began to shout, 'There's a finch on Tom Duggan's sprig. Quick, Tom, quick.'

But my father had already burst through the bushes and was tearing across the field, his big boots shaking the earth. The charm rose in a coloured cloud at his coming and flew off twittering to the west.

My father flung himself to his knees beside the trapped bird and we could see his shoulders moving as he took it from the sprig.

And then, instead of running back to us, he remained kneeling there, his body petrified, his head bowed to the ground. The men of our parish shifted their feet angrily as they began to shout at him. 'What's wrong with you, man? Wake up, Tom, and don't be falling asleep on the job. Will you hurry on the hell out of there!'

The cobbler turned and glared at them. 'Fair play for the Glenbay Trapper,' he roared. 'The contest isn't over yet.'

Puzzled I stared at the bent stiff figure of my father and then I heard the twittering in the sky and I looked up. A solitary goldfinch, a straggler from the charm, was dipping towards the field. The Glenbay bird burst into song and he dived to greet him. He circled the cage twice and perched on the limed twig. I closed my eyes tight as I saw the Glenbay Trapper charging across the field. When I opened them he was putting the trapped bird into the cobbler's hand and the shouting of the delighted Glenbay men was cracking the sky. I turned away from them and ran like mad to my father, the tears streaming down my face.

'Faad,' I cried, 'Oh! Fadd, what happened you? Are you sick or what?' He opened his fist and showed me a goldfinch lying limp in his palm.

'I killed him,' he said sadly. 'God forgive me, I killed the little fellow taking him from the sprig.'

I groped around for words to say something comforting to him but I couldn't find any. The Glenbay trapper came swaggering across to us and my father gave him our call-bird. 'You were unlucky to lose, Tom,' he told my father.

He went back to his friends and they marched down the road to their own parish, cheering loudly. I stood beside my father among the purple thistles and we looked after them until the cheering died away.

The Boy who had no Story

Kevin Danaher

*T*here was a young fellow from this parish long ago, and it was always said that there was no great welcome before him in the house where he would go of an evening, because you might as well have a rock of bogdeal stuck up in the corner as to have himself, for he was dumb in any sort of entertainment, without a song or a story or even a handful of riddles in his head.

He used to travel away down the County Limerick, working for the farmers, and he used to put up here and there along the road, and before long he noticed that he was not very welcome, for although people were hospitable to the stranger, they expected him to have all the latest news or to keep the night going with a song or a story. Poor Paddy was heart-scalded, but what could he do, the poor fellow?

Well, one night he was going along a lonely part of the road, and he saw this light in a house inside in the fields, and he made for it. It was a queer dark big-looking house, and the door was opened by a queer dark big-looking man.

'Welcome, Paddy Ahern,' says the man. 'Come on in and take a seat at the fire.'

Paddy could not make out how the man knew his name, but he was too much in dread to say anything, for it was a very queer place. They had the supper, and the man showed Paddy where to sleep, and he stretched himself out, tired after the road.

But it was not much rest he got. He was hardly asleep when the door burst open, and in with three men and they dragging a coffin after them. There was no sign of the man of the house.

'Who will help us to carry the coffin?' says the first of the men to the other two.

'Who but Paddy Ahern?' says they.

Poor Paddy had to get up and throw on his clothes, and he was shaking with the fright. He had to go under the feet of the coffin with one of the men, and the other two went under the head. Off with them out the door and away across the fields. It was not long until poor Paddy was all wet and dirty from falling into dikes and all torn and scratched from pulling through hedges and ditches. Every time he stopped they abused him, and a few times he fell they held kicking him until he got up again. He was in a terrible way. Finally they came to a graveyard, a frightening lonesome-looking place with a high wall around it.

'Who will take the coffin in over the wall?' says the first man.

'Who but Paddy Ahern?' says they.

Poor Paddy had to lift the coffin in over the wall, although it nearly bested him. He was hardly able to stand by this time. But they would not let him take a rest.

'Who will dig the grave?' says the first man.

'Who will dig it but Paddy Ahern?' says they.

They gave him a spade and a shovel and made him dig the grave.

'Who will open the coffin?' says the first man.

'Who will open it but Paddy Ahern?' says the other two.

He was nearly fainting with the terror, but he had to go down on his knee and take off the screws and lift the cover. And do you know what? The coffin was empty, although it was frightful weight to carry.

'Who will go in the coffin?' says the first man.

'Who will go in but Paddy Ahern?' says they.

They made a drive for poor Paddy, but if they did, he didn't wait for them, but away out with him over the wall in one leap and away across the country, and the three after him with every screech out of them and every halloo, the same as if it was a hunt. They nearly had him caught more than once, but he managed to keep out in front of them, until he saw a light in a window. Paddy made for it and he shouting at the top of his voice to the people of the house to come and save him. But who should open the door but the queer dark big-looking man? That was too much for poor Paddy; he fell in around the kitchen in a dead faint.

When he recovered his senses, it was broad daylight, and the queer man was up and working around the kitchen. There was not a sign of anyone else in the house.

'You are awake, Paddy?' says the man of the house. 'Did you have a good night's sleep?'

'Go bhfóiridh Dia orainn,' says poor Paddy, 'but I did not. It is destroyed I am after all the hardship I had to put up with during the night! And not one single minute longer will I stay in this house, but to be legging it away as quick as I can!'

He got up and put on his clothes, and would you believe it—there was no sign of the night's hardship on them. They were his old working clothes, of course, but they were clean enough and dry. He did not know what to make of it.

'Now, listen to me, Paddy Ahern,' says the man of the house. 'It was how I was sorry for the way you were going the road, without a story or a song in your head. But tell me this much now – haven't you a fine adventure story to be telling in every house you go to, after last night?'

Not a word out of poor Paddy, but to grab up his stick and his bundle and away with him as quick as his legs could carry him. And whatever look he gave back and he crossing the ditch to the main road, there was not a house nor a sign of one to be seen, but only the bare fields and a few cows grazing in them.

The Tinker of Ballingarry and his Three Wishes

Jeremiah Curtin

In Ballingarry, County of Limerick, there lived once a tinker named Jack. All tinkers are poor and so was Jack; still he was not so poor as another, for he had a small green garden behind his cottage and a fine apple tree in it. Jack travelled the country nearly all the time and left his wife to mind the cottage and garden.

One day while on the road with his pack he met a very 'dacent' looking man and saluted him respectfully. The stranger was pleased with the tinker, and said:

'Three wishes will be given you. You can ask for three things. You will get whatever you ask for. Do the best you can. You will never have a chance like this again.'

Jack thought and said: 'I have a strong armchair in my house. Whoever comes in sits down in that chair and I have to stand. I wish now that every one who sits on the chair from this out to grow fast to it, and the chair to be fast to the ground, and no man to have power to rise from the chair till I say the word.'

'Granted,' said the man. 'Now tell your second wish, and 'tis my advice to you to wish for something that will be of service – something that will do you good.'

Jack thought awhile and said: 'In my garden there is a tree which bears beautiful apples, but all the small boys and little blackguards of the country steal every one of them and I never have one to eat. I wish every person who tries to steal an apple from that tree to be fastened to the apple and the apple to the tree and to have the person hung there till freed by me.'

'Granted,' said the man. 'Now is your third and last chance. I advise you for the last time. Wish for something of service. Be careful and get something that will be of use to you.'

Jack thought and thought, and then said:

'My wife has a leather bag: in that bag she puts scraps of wool that the neighbours give her when she works for them. Now, the small boys and blackguards of the country come to my house, kick this bag around, pull the wool out and waste it. I wish everything that goes into the bag to stay in it till I give the word to go out.'

'Granted,' said the man, 'but, my poor fellow, you have done ill for yourself.'

The fine-looking gentleman went his way travelling, and Jack the tinker went home happy, but as poor as before.

Some time after Jack met with an accident, and lay at home a whole year. He was at death's door from hunger, when a stranger walked the way one day and said to him:

'I see, my poor man, that you are very poor and in need. You are hungry. I am ready to make a bargain with you. I will give you comfort and make a rich man of you if you will come with me at the end of seven years.'

'Your offer is very enticing. Who are you?' asked Jack.

'Who am I?' repeated the stranger. 'To make a long story short, I'm the Devil.'

'No matter, your honour, who you are. I'll take your offer.' And Jack promised to be ready to go with the stranger at the end of seven years.

The Devil went away, and Jack was very rich for a tinker. There was no lack of food in his house: there was plenty from that out, and to spare. He went tinkering no longer from place to place, or if he did itself it was for his own pleasure. His wife went wool-picking for the neighbours no longer. They remained in their cottage, and all went well with the tinker and his wife, to the great surprise of the people around.

Jack soon forgot about the Devil and the promise that he had given him. The seven years passed quickly; the last day of the last year came, and the stranger stood before Jack.

'The seven years are up,' said he. 'Come with me; I have done my part, now you must do yours.'

'A promise is a promise,' said Jack. 'I'll go with you; I am well satisfied. But do you sit in this chair awhile, and wait for me: I'll not delay long. As I am leaving the wife forever, I'd like to say a last word to her. I'll be back in a minute and go with you.'

The Devil sat down in Jack's chair, and waited.

Jack was not long in giving goodbye to his wife, and said: 'I am ready; let us start.'

The Devil tried to rise, but, pull and jerk as he might, he could not move from the chair nor stir the chair from the ground. He let a screech out of him that was heard over three townlands, and struggled terribly, but no use for him, he could not rise. Seeing that he was fast and that there was no escape for him, he said to Jack: 'I'll give you twice as much wealth and fourteen years to enjoy it if you will release me.'

'I am satisfied,' said Jack. 'Up and away with you.'

The Devil shot away like a dart of lightning. Now Jack was twice as rich as before, but he made no show of his wealth. He lived in the same little cottage.

The fourteen years passed as quickly as the seven, for Jack had twice as much to spend. The time was up again, and the Devil was at the front door. He was very watchful this time, and said to the tinker:

'You'll play me no tricks now. Get ready and come.'

Jack made ready quickly. The day was hot and when they were ready to start, Jack said:

'We may as well go through my garden. Many is the pleasant hour I spent in it. Now that I am never to pass another day there, I would like a last look at the place.'

The Devil consented, sure of Jack this time. They walked through the garden to the end of it, where there was a large tree laden with beautiful apples.

'The day is hot,' said Jack, 'the journey before us is a long one. You are taller than I. Pluck some of those nice apples; they will be good on the road.'

'I will do the same,' said the Devil, and springing, he caught a large apple, but he could neither pull off the apple nor loosen his hold on it. There he was swinging from the tree. He shouted and screeched, struggled and pulled, but no use for him.

'Take me down out of this,' said he.

'Indeed, then, I will not; you may stay there till the day of judgment, for anything I care.'

'You'll have no luck in your house if you leave me here,' said the Devil.

'Luck or no luck,' said Jack, 'I'd rather have you there than go with you.'

'Well,' said the Devil at last, 'I will give you three times the wealth you had at first and twenty-one years to enjoy it in if you will loosen me.'

Jack thought a while, and then said to himself: 'It is better to let him off than to have him here near me. He might do me some harm though he is in the tree.' So Jack freed the Devil from the apple tree, and away he went without delay.

Jack had wealth and plenty for twenty-one years; whatever he wished for he had. At the end the Devil stood before him and said: 'You'll play me no trick this turn, and when I have you in my kingdom I'll pay you for what you have done to me; I'll be even with you there.'

'I'll have to take my chances with you, I suppose,' said Jack, 'but let me say goodbye to my wife now.'

'Very well,' said the Devil.

Jack went to his wife, took the wool bag, and started. The two walked forward quickly. Jack was silent a long time; at last he said to the Devil: 'I have been thinking of the time when I was a little boy and the children of the village and I used to play a trick together. I was very nimble in those days, but now I am old and heavy. I brought this bag with me to remind me of my boyhood.' He took out the bag and, showing it to the Devil, said:

'I used to jump in and out of this bag, I was so fit and active.'

'Oh, what sort of a trick is that?' said the Devil. 'That's no trick at all.'

'Well,' said Jack, 'I don't think you can do it, and I'll never believe you can till I see you.'

He held the bag open; the Devil sprang in. Jack closed the bag in an instant, and said:

'Now you are in and I'll never let you out.'

In spite of the howling inside Jack put the bag on his back and went on. The Devil begged and begged.

'Oh, let me out,' cried he to Jack, but Jack would not listen to him.

In a couple of hours the tinker came to a place where four men were thrashing grain with flails.

'I have a bag here that's too thick and stiff to carry. Will you give it a few blows? Make it limber for me,' said he.

The men walloped the bag. It hopped like a ball. They flailed it till they broke their flails.

'Take that bag out of this,' cried the men. 'The

Devil himself must be in it.'

'Oh, then,' said Jack, 'maybe it's himself that's in it, sure enough.'

He travelled on with the bag on his shoulders; the Devil was begging and promising at every step of the journey.

'No,' said Jack, 'I'll never let you out again to do harm in the world. I will pay you for your work.'

Jack found a tucking mill, and going to the owner, said: 'I want to thicken this bag a little, will you let it go through the mill?'

'Oh, why not,' said the man.

Jack threw the bag in; the man was surprised at the cracking and smashing and terrible noise in the bag. After a while what happened to the mill but to break.

'Out of that! I am beggared entirely; my mill is in bits. Out o' that with your bag, it must be the Devil that's in it!'

'Sure and maybe that's the truth you're telling,' said Jack, taking the bag and walking off with it.

After a while he came to a forge; four strong men were at work with four sledges on a great piece of iron.

'The day is hot,' said Jack, 'and my bag is weighty and stiff. Will you give it a few blows of the sledge for me?'

The men winked at one another, as much as to say, we'll make bits of the bag for him.

'Why not?' said they.

Jack threw down the bag; the four men went at it, gave it many a good blow; each time they struck the bag flew to the top of the forge. The men worked till tired and panting; then called out: 'Away with your bag; it must be the Devil himself that's in it!'

The foreman, angry at the loss of time and work, caught a hot iron from the fire and punched the bag with it. The iron went into the Devil's eye and destroyed it. He howled and screamed.

'Let me out! Let me out! I promise never to come in your way. I will not have you in my kingdom. I'll leave you alone forever. I'll give you riches for four times as long as at first.'

At last Jack opened the bag and let him out. Away flew the Devil, and was soon out of sight.

Jack went home now a free man, with plenty to eat and drink for twenty-eight years. But the twenty-eight years passed quickly, and Jack, being a tinker, could never save a penny. He was very old, and after the end of the twenty-eight years he was very poor. His day came at last and he went to the other world. He stood at the door of the good place and knocked.

'Go to the one you worked for all your life. You cannot come here,' was the answer.

Jack went and rapped at the gate of the bad place. They asked: 'Who's there?'

'Jack the tinker, from Ballingarry.'

'Oh, don't let him in!' screamed a voice: 'don't let him in! He put me eye out; he will destroy every one of us.'

There was fear and trembling at the sound of Jack's voice. He could get no admittance to that place at any price. The tinker went back to the gate of the good place. He could not enter, but sentence was passed to let him travel the world forever and carry a small lantern at night. He was to have no rest, but wander over bogs, marshes, moors, and lonely places and lead people astray.

He is roaming and travelling, and will be in that way till the day of judgment.

People know him as Jack the Lantern.

The Ghost of the Valley

Lord Dunsany

I went for a walk one evening under old willows whose pollarded trunks leaned over a little stream. A mist lay over the stream and filled the valley far over the heads of the willows and hid the feet of the hills. And higher than that I saw a pillar of mist stand up above the level of the grass slopes, where they ended under the edge of the darkening woods. So strange it seemed standing there in the dim of the evening, that I moved nearer to see it, which I could not clearly do where I was, nearly a hundred yards away, because of the rest of the mist; but as I moved towards it, and less and less of the river mist was between us, I saw it clearer and clearer, till I stood at the feet of that tall diaphanous figure.

One by one lights appeared where there had been none before: for it was that hour when the approach of night is noticed in cottages, and the flower-like glow of windows here and there was adding a beauty and mystery to the twilight. In the great loneliness there, with no one to speak to, standing before that towering figure of mist that was as lonely as I, I should have liked to have spoken to it. And then there came to me the odd thought. Why not? There was no one to hear me, and it need not answer.

So I said 'What are you?' and so small and shrill was the answer, that at first I thought it was birds of the reeds and water that spoke. 'A ghost,' it seemed to be saying. 'What?' said I. And then more clearly it said, 'Have you never seen ghosts before?'

I said that I never had, and it seemed to lose interest in me. To regain its attention if possible, I said that I had sometimes seen strange things in the twilight which very likely were ghosts, although I did not know it at the time. And there seemed to come back into the tall grey figure some slight increase of intensity, as though its lost interest were slowly returning, and in tones that sounded scornful of my ignorance it said 'They probably were.'

'And you?' I inquired again.

'The ghost of this valley,' it said.

'Always?' I asked.

'Not always,' it said. 'Little more than a thousand years. My father was the smoke of one of those cottages and my mother was the mist over the stream. She of course was here always.'

It was strange to hear so tall a figure talking with so tiny a voice: had a waterhen been uttering its shrill cry near me it would have drowned the voice of the ghost, which barely emerged from the chatter of waterfowl further away.

'What was it like in this valley,' I asked, 'when you were young?'

For a while the tall shape said nothing, and seemed to be indolently turning its head, as though it looked from side to side of the valley. 'The heads of the willows were not cut,' it said. 'But that was when I was very young. They were cut off soon after. And there were not so many cottages. Not nearly so many, and they were all of thatch at first. They lit their fires all through the autumn. My mother loved the autumn: it is to us what spring is to you. My father rose up then from one of the chimneys, high over the thatch, and the wind drifted him and so they met. He remembered the talk of the firesides long ago, but only a few centuries more than a thousand years. My mother can remember for ever. She remembers when there were no huts here and no men. She remembers what was, and knows what is coming.'

'I don't want to hear about that,' I said.

Something like a cackle of laughter seemed to escape from the ghost. But it may have been only the quacking of far-off ducks, which were fighting at that hour.

'What do you do yourself?' I asked.

'I drift,' it said, 'whenever there is wind. Like you.'

'Drift!' I said. 'We don't drift. We have our policies.' I was about to explain them to the ghost, when it interrupted.

'You all drift before them helplessly,' it said. 'You and your friends and your enemies.'

'It is easy for you to criticise,' I answered.

'I am not criticising,' it said. 'I am just as helpless. I drift this way and that upon any wind. I can no more control the winds than you can turn Destiny.'

'Nonsense,' I said. 'We are masters of all Creation. We have made inventions which you would never understand down there by your river and the smoke of the cottages.'

'But you have to live with them,' it said.

'And you?' I asked.

'I am going,' it said.

'Why?' I asked it.

'Times are changing,' it said. 'The old firesides are altering, and they are poisoning the river, and the smoke of the cities is unwholesome, like your bread. I am going away among unicorns, griffins and wyverns.'

'But are there such things?' I asked.

'There used to be,' it replied.

But I was growing impatient at being lectured by a ghost, and was a little chilled by the mist.

'Are there such things as ghosts?' I asked then.

And a wind blew then and the ghost was suddenly gone.

'We used to be,' it sighed softly.

Godfather Death

Gerard Murphy

Con O'Leary was looking for a godfather for his child. None of those that offered themselves satisfied him; for he found them partial and apt to favour their friends at the expense of others. Finally, a tall thin man came to the door.

'I hear you are looking for a godfather for your child,' said the tall man.

'I am,' said the father. 'But I'll have nobody partial or unfair. Who are you?'

'My name is Death,' said the tall thin man.

'If you're Death,' said the father, 'I need look no further. For there is no one so impartial as Death. You strike them all alike, without fear or favour. Will you be godfather to my child?'

'I will,' said Death. And the child was baptised.

'Now, you've done me an honour,' said Death, 'and I'll tell you something in return that may help you. Whenever you go to a sick person's bedside you'll see me in the room. If I am at the sick person's head, the sick person will die; but if I am at the sick person's feet, the sick person will recover.'

A few days later, Con O'Leary heard that a neighbour was ill. He went to visit him. He asked the woman of the house how her husband was.

'He's badly, Con,' said the woman of the house.

'Might I see him?' Con asked.

'I'm afraid not,' said the woman. 'The priest and the doctor have been here and they said that no one should be let visit him.'

'If he's as bad as that, I'm all the more anxious to see him,' said Con. 'Would you mind telling him I'm here.'

The woman told her husband that Con O'Leary had arrived and was very anxious to speak to him. 'Send him in,' said the sick man.

Con went in 'You're welcome, Con,' said the sick man.

'Long life to you,' said Con. 'How do you feel yourself?'

'Very bad,' said the sick man. 'It won't be long till I'm dead.'

'You're not going to die this time,' said Con; for he had seen Death standing at the sick man's feet. 'Get a drink of whey,' said Con to the sick man's wife. The wife brought the whey. Con put his arm around the sick man's shoulders and helped him to sit up. 'Drink this,' he said, putting the whey to the sick man's lips.

The sick man drank the whey. 'You'll see that you'll be all right in a few days' time,' said Con. 'I'll come again myself tomorrow.'

The next day, Con came again to the sick man's house.

'You are welcome, Con,' said the woman of the house. 'He's much better today.'

'Put out your tongue,' said Con to the sick man. 'It is my opinion,' said Con after he had examined the sick man's tongue, 'that you'll be doing your work as well as ever you were before a week is out.'

Con was right in his opinion, and soon everyone was saying that Con O'Leary was as good as any doctor and better than most.

A rich lord, who live ten miles away, fell ill. He sent his coach to Con O'Leary's house to fetch him to his bedside.

'Oh! I couldn't go so far from home,' said Con, 'unless I were well paid for it.'

'You'll get whatever you ask,' said the coachman.

When Con came to the rich man's bedside, he saw the tall thin man standing by his head. Con felt the sick man's pulse and looked at his tongue. 'You're as bad as a man could be,' he said.

'Is there no hope?' asked the lord.

Con thought for a few moments. 'You're lying the wrong way for your health,' he said. 'First we must turn you round the right way in the bed.' They moved the lord round in the bed so that his feet were where his head had been. Then Con went out to the garden and gathered some herbs. He made a cooling drink of the herbs and gave it to the sick man. The sick man began to get better at once. That afternoon, he was able to sit up. He kept Con in the house for a week, treating him as if he were a great doctor. He then paid him a huge fee, and sent him home in the coach.

When Con arrived home, the tall thin man was waiting for him. 'No one can play tricks with Death,' said the tall man. 'You must come with me now.'

'Very well,' said Con; and they set off together. Death walked with him towards the sea. When they reached the sea, Con asked Death for a few minutes' respite while he smoked his last pipe and drank his last drink. Death granted his last request. Con took his pipe and a half-empty whiskey bottle from his pocket. He offered Death a drink. Death drank some of the whiskey and Con drank what was left. They chattered while Con filled his pipe.

'My father was very clever with tricks,' said Con.

'What could he do?' asked Death.

'His best trick,' said Con, 'was jumping into a bottle no bigger than a whiskey-bottle.'

'That's easy,' said Death.

'Well, all I'll say,' said Con, 'is that it's something you could never do.'

'Show me the bottle,' said Death.

Con placed the bottle on the ground in front of Death. Death jumped into the bottle. When he was safely in, Con fixed the cork in the mouth of the bottle, and threw the bottle far out to sea.

For seven years no one died, for Death was closed up in the bottle being tossed about by the waves. At the end of seven years, the waves cast the bottle on the beach. A boy found it and drew out the cork. Death was free once more. He walked straight to Con O'Leary's house. This time Con O'Leary had to go. In spite of his cleverness, Death was too strong for him in the end.

The Captain in the Box

J M Synge

*T*here were two farmers in County Clare. One had a son, and the other, a fine rich man, had a daughter.

The young man was wishing to marry the girl, and his father told him to try and get her if he thought well, though a power of gold would be wanting to get the like of her.

'I will try,' said the young man.

He put all his gold into a bag. Then he went over to the other farm, and threw in the gold in front of him.

'Is that all gold?' said the father of the girl.

'All gold,' said O'Conor (the young man's name was O'Conor).

'It will not weigh down my daughter,' said the father.

'We'll see that,' said O'Conor.

Then they put them in the scales, the daughter in the one side and the gold in the other. The girl went down against the ground, so O'Conor took his bag and went out on the road.

As he was going along he came to where there was a little man, and he standing with his back against the wall.

69

'Where are you going with the bag?' asked the little man.

'Going home,' said O'Conor.

'Is it gold you might be wanting?' said the man.

'It is surely,' said O'Conor.

'I'll give you what you are wanting,' said the man, 'and we can bargain in this way – you'll pay me back in the year the gold I give you or you'll pay me back in a year with five pounds cut off your own flesh.'

That bargain was made between them. The man gave a bag of gold to O'Conor, and he went back with it and was married to the young woman.

They were rich people, and he built her a grand castle on the cliffs of Clare, with a window that looked out straightly over the wild ocean.

One day when he went up with his wife to look out over at the wild ocean, he saw a ship coming in on the rocks, and no sails on her at all. She was wrecked on the rocks, and it was tea that was in her, and fine silk.

O'Conor and his wife went down to look at the wreck, and when the lady O'Conor saw the silk she said she wished a dress of it.

They got the silk from the sailors, and when the Captain came up to get the money for it, O'Conor asked him to come again and take his dinner with them. They had a grand dinner, and they drank after it, and the Captain was tipsy. While they were still drinking a letter came to O'Conor, and it was in the letter that a friend of his was dead, and that he would have to go away on a long journey. As he was getting ready the Captain came to him.

'Are you fond of your wife?' said the Captain.

'I am fond her,' said O'Conor.

'Will you make me a bet of twenty guineas no man comes near her while you'll be away on the journey?' said the Captain.

'I will bet it,' said O'Conor, and he went away.

There was an old hag who sold small things on the road near the castle, and the lady O'Conor allowed her to sleep up in her room in a big box. The Captain went down on the road to the old hag.

'For how much will you let me sleep one night in your box?' said the Captain.

'For no money at all would I do such a thing,' said the hag.

'For ten guineas?' said the Captain.

'Not for ten guineas,' said the hag.

'For twelve guineas?' said the Captain.

'Not for twelve guineas,' said the hag.

'For fifteen guineas,' said the Captain.

'For fifteen I will do it,' said the hag.

Then she took him up and hid him in the box. When night came the lady O'Conor walked up into her room, and the Captain watched her through a hole that was in the box. He saw her take off her two rings and put them on a kind of board that was over her head like a chimney-piece, and take off her clothes, except her shift, and go up into her bed.

As soon as she was asleep the Captain came out of the box, and he had some means of making a light, for he lit the candle. He went over to the bed where she was sleeping without disturbing her at all, or doing any bad thing, and he took the two rings off the board, and blew out the light, and

71

went down again into the box.

When O'Conor came back the Captain met him, and told him that he had been a night in his wife's room, and gave him the two rings.

O'Conor gave him the twenty guineas of the bet. Then he went up into the castle, and he took his wife up to look out of the window out over the wild ocean. While she was looking he pushed from behind, and she fell down over the cliff into the sea.

An old woman was on the shore, and she saw her falling. She went down then to the surf and pulled her out all wet and in great disorder, and she took the wet clothes off of her, and put on some old rags belonging to herself.

When O'Conor had pushed his wife from the window he went away into the land.

After a while the lady O'Conor went out searching for him, and when she had gone here and there a long time in the country, she heard that he was reaping in a field with sixty men.

She came to the field and she wanted to go in, but the gate-man would not open the gate for her. Then the owner came by, and her husband was there, reaping, but he never gave any sign of knowing her. She showed him to the owner, and he made the man come out and go with his wife.

Then the lady O'Conor took him out on the road where there were horses, and they rode away. When they came to the place where O'Conor had met the little man, he was there on the road before him.

'Have you my gold on you?' said the man.

'I have not,' said O'Conor.

'Then you'll pay me the flesh off your body,' said the man.

They went into the house, and a knife was brought, and a clean white cloth was put on the table, and O'Conor was put on the table.

Then the little man was going to strike the lancet into him, when says lady O'Conor –

'Have you bargained for five pounds of flesh?'

'For five pounds of flesh,' said the man.

'Have you bargained for any drop of his blood?' said lady O'Conor.

'For no blood,' said the man.

'Cut out the flesh,' said lady O'Conor, 'but if you spill one drop of his blood I'll put that through you.' And she put a pistol to his head.

The little man went away and they saw no more of him.

When they got home to their castle they made a great supper, and they invited the Captain and the old hag, and the old woman that had pulled the lady O'Conor out of the sea.

After they had eaten well the lady O'Conor began, and she said they would all tell their stories. Then she told how she had been saved from the sea, and how she had found her husband.

Then the old woman told her story, the way she had found the lady O'Conor wet, and in great disorder, and had brought her in and put on her some old rags of her own.

The lady O'Conor asked the Captain for his story, but he said they would get no story from him. The she took her pistol out of her pocket, and she put it on the edge of the table, and she said that

73

any one that did not tell his story would get a bullet into him.

Then the Captain told the way he had got into the box, and come over to her bed without touching her at all, and had taken away the rings.

Then the lady O'Conor took the pistol; and shot the hag through the body, and they threw her over the cliff into the sea.

The Black Chafer

Pádraig Pearse

*I*t was a tramp from the Joyce country who came into our house one wild wintry night that told us the story of the 'Black Chafer' as we sat around the fire.

The wind was wailing around the house, like women keening the dead, as he was speaking, and he made his voice rise or fall according as the wind rose or fell.

He was a tall man with wild eyes and his clothes were almost in tatters. In a way, I was afraid of him, when I first saw him, and his story did nothing to lessen that fear.

'The three most blessed animals in the world,' he said, 'are the haddock, the robin and the lady-bird. And the three most cursed animals are the snake, the wren and the black chafer. And the black chafer is the most cursed of them all.

'I know that only too well. If a man should kill your son, woman of the house, never call him a black chafer, or if a woman should come between you and your husband, don't compare her with the black chafer.'

'God save us,' my mother said.

'Amen,' he replied.

The tramp didn't speak again for a long time. We all stayed quiet because we knew he was going to tell us a story. It wasn't long before he began.

When I was a boy (he began), there was a woman in our village that everyone was afraid of. She lived in a little lonely cabin in a mountain-gap and nobody would ever go near her house. Neither would she come near anyone's house herself. Nobody would speak to her when they met her on the road, and she never stopped to talk with anyone either.

You would have pity for the creature just to see her walking the roads by herself, alone.

'Who is she,' I used to ask my mother, 'or why won't they speak to her?'

'Shh-hh- boy,' she always replied. 'That's the Black Chafer, a woman with a curse on her.'

'What did she do or who put the curse on her?'

'She was cursed by a priest, they say, but nobody knows what she did.'

And that's all the information I could get about her until I was a grown chap. Even then, I could find out nothing, except that she committed some dreadful sin, when she was young, and that she was cursed publicly by a priest on account of it. One Sunday, when the people were assembled at Mass, the priest turned around and said from the altar:

'There is a woman here that will merit eternal damnation for herself and for every person friendly with her. And I say to that woman, that she is a cursed woman, and I say to you, to be as neighbourly to her as you would be to a black chafer.'

'Then he said: "Rise up now, Black Chafer, and avoid the company of decent people from this out!"

The poor woman got up and went out of the chapel. She was never called anything after that, except The Black Chafer, and her real name was soon forgotten. It was said that she had the evil eye. If she ever looked on a calf or sheep that wasn't her own, the animals died. Before long, the women were afraid to let their children out on the village street if she was passing by.

I married a very attractive girl when I was twenty-one. We had a little girl and were expecting another child. One day when I was cutting turf on the bog my wife was feeding hens in the street, when she saw – God between us and harm – the Black Chafer coming up the bohereen carrying the girl in her arms. One of the child's arms was woven around the women's neck, and her shawl covered the mite's body. My wife was speechless!

The Black Chafer laid the little girl in her mother's arms and my wife noticed that her clothes were wet.

'What happened the child?' she asked.

'She was looking for water-lilies around the Pool of the Rushes when she fell in,' the woman replied. 'I was crossing the road when I heard her screaming. I jumped over the ditch and managed to catch her just in the nick of time.'

'May God reward you,' said my wife. The other woman went off before she had time to say anymore. My wife brought the child inside, dried her and put her to bed. When I came home from the bog she told me what happened. We both prayed for the Black Chafer that night.

The following day, the little girl began to prattle

about the woman that saved her. 'The water was in my mouth, and in my eyes and in my ears,' she told us, 'I saw shining sparks and heard a great noise; I was slipping and slipping and suddenly I felt a hand about me, and she lifted me up and kissed me. I thought I was at home when I was in her arms with her shawl around me.'

A few days after that, my wife discovered that the child was missing. She was missing for a couple of hours. When she came home, she told us that she was after paying a visit to the woman who saved her life. 'She made a cake for me,' she told us. 'There is nobody in the house but herself so I promised her I'd call in to see her every day.'

Neither my wife nor I could say a word against her. The Black Chafer was after saving the girl's life so it wouldn't have been natural to prevent her from going up to the lonely house in the gap of the mountain. From that day onwards the child went up the hill to see her every evening.

The neighbours told us that it wasn't right. In a way we knew that we were wrong, but how could we help it?

Would you believe me, friends? From the day the Black Chafer laid eyes on the little girl she began to dwindle and dwindle like a fire that couldn't be rekindled! She soon lost her appetite and strength and after three months she was only a shadow. A month later she was in the churchyard.

The Black Chafer came down the mountain the day she was buried. They wouldn't let her into the graveyard. She turned back sorrowfully and slowly traced her footsteps up to the mountain path again.

I pitied the poor creature, because I knew that our trouble was no heavier than her own.

The next morning I went up the mountain path myself. I meant to tell her that neither my wife nor myself bore her any grudge or blamed her for what had happened. I knocked at her door but got no answer. I went in and saw that the ashes were red on the hearth. There was nobody at all to be seen. Then I noticed a bed in the corner of the room, so I went over to it. The Black Chafer was lying on it ... cold and dead.

From that day onwards my household and myself have been plagued with disaster. My wife died in childbirth a month afterwards. The baby didn't survive. My cattle picked up some disease the following winter and the landlord put me out of my holding. I have been travelling the roads of Connacht, as a walking man, ever since.

Neilly and the Fir Tree

John O'Connor

*N*eilly watched dreamily as the boy in the red jersey dropped from the big fir-tree back on to the ground again. The rest of the boys gathered round calling out questions, but Neilly didn't move. He stood with his hands behind his back, a look of sadness in his large hazel eyes.

The boy in the red jersey shook his head, obviously very thankful to be back on firm ground again.

'It's no good! Nobody'll ever be able to climb that tree.'

He was the third to have attempted it. Two of the others had already tried, but they also had failed. The boy in the red jersey had the name of being the best climber of them all, and now that the big fir tree had beaten him too, well it didn't seem much good for anyone else to try.

He shook his head again. 'Nobody'll ever be able to climb that tree ... You might be able to get *past* that part all right, but you'd never be able to get back down again. You'd be stuck there all night. Isn't that right Franky?'

All the boys walked backwards out into the field, staring upwards, until halfway up the tree, they could see the bare part like a faint magic girdle encircling the trunk. Here for a space of about six or seven feet the trunk was devoid of any branches. The boys argued and shook their heads. No one took the slightest notice of little Neilly standing a few yards away.

There were three firs standing on top of the hill. Like three monuments erected by some long-vanished race, they towered up into the air, a landmark for miles around.

Neilly gave a faint shudder as he looked up into the fir. He felt so terribly small and insignificant beside this glowering monster. Neilly was a small slight lad of about nine. He was easily the youngest and smallest of the entire group. His legs and arms were slender as reeds, and he wore a pair of ponderous looking black boots – no stockings. His right boot was soaking wet, and smeared with pale, gluey mud. That was where he had nearly fallen into St Bridget's drain, about ten minutes ago. Everyone else had jumped it except him. Poor Neilly! How he wished he were a bit bigger, so that he could jump and climb as well as the other lads. It wasn't his fault that he was so small, but the rest of the boys didn't think of that. When they did anything that he couldn't, they just jeered at him, or worse even – ignored him altogether. Neilly suddenly became aware of his companions glances.

The boy in the red jersey was pointing at him dramatically.

'There you are !' he shouted. 'I bet you Neilly could climb it though. Couldn't you Neilly?'

'Ah, he can't even jump St Bridget's drain, yet, even,' another boy chimed in. At this Neilly bit his lip, hiding his wet, muddy boot behind his dry left one.

The boys came closer.

'Ah, poor wee Neilly! What are you blushing

about, Neilly? What are you blushing about?'

The boy in the red jersey stuck his hands up.

'I still say that Neilly could climb that tree.' He put his hand on Neilly's shoulder. 'Couldn't you Neilly?'

Neilly shook the hand off instantly. The boy gave him a push, and then the rest of the boys began pushing him too. Neilly became infuriated. He made a wild swing with his boot, but the boys only jeered louder. Neilly's rage increased. He broke through his tormentors, and rushed over to the fir.

'For two pins I would climb your ould tree for you,' he raged. 'Do you think I couldn't, like?'

The jeering grew louder. The boys were enjoying themselves immensely. With a mighty effort Neilly forced himself to be calm. He turned to the tree. The lower part of the enormous trunk was worn smooth and shiny, where the cows had come to scratch. Neilly stripped off his boots, then, standing on a great, humpbacked root, he gave a great jump, reaching for a huge rusty staple which was driven into the trunk about five feet off the ground. He caught it, skinning his knee against the bark. He made another lunge towards the first branch a little higher, and drew himself up, casting a swift, triumphant glance at the boys below.

As he climbed he became filled with joy. The rich spicy scent of resin hung in the air like incense, and his hands and feet grew rough and sticky, which, of course, made his progress all the more easy.

Now and then he glanced through the heavy green foliage. The fields seemed a great distance below, but the thrill he felt was one of daring rather than fear. He could hear the faint sound of his name being called by the boys below. But he urged on, too excited to answer.

He came at last to the bare part, and here, craning up, he caught his breath in dismay. Except for a few withered branches, the column of the tree was bare indeed. Above, near enough to mock him, but far enough to frighten him, the heavy growth of the tree resumed. In some past storm perhaps, a sabre of lightening had put its brand here, killing the branches but leaving the bole itself unharmed.

With a sinking heart Neilly circled the tree, searching for a reliable grip, but there was nothing except those few, puny branches, and they looked too frail to bear even his weight.

It would be terrible to have to turn back now. For a moment he felt like risking all in one mad hopeless leap for the foliage above. Then a look of fierce determination settled on his face.

One of the stricken branches grew just within reach of his fingers. He gripped it cautiously, as near to the trunk as possible. He pressed gingerly and it gave a few ominous creaks. The pounding of his heart increased. Gradually he pulled at the branch until at last his entire weight was drooping from it. Hardly daring to breathe, he prised himself up inch by inch, and then grabbed frantically at another branch higher up. He closed his eyes fully expecting it to snap, but although it gave a loud, terrifying creak and shivered alarmingly, it held. Panting, he struggled up until he was able to stand on the bottom branch.

For a minute he hugged the trunk afraid to move another inch. The rough, scenty bole of the fir, seemed the most beautiful thing in the world. Then, fearfully, he allowed his eyes to creep upwards. Tremblingly, he reached up with his right hand, scraping it over the bark, but six inches separated his fingers from the lowermost living branch. He glanced down at the rotten branch he was standing on, and his head began to spin. For a time he stood pressed against the trunk, groaning softly to himself.

Then he looked up and reached his hand out again. He eased himself gently away from the trunk, keeping his eyes fixed as though by hypnotism on the branch above. The tip of his tongue stuck out. His legs bent slightly. Then he *sprang*.

With a loud crack, the branch below him broke off, but at the same time the fingers of his right hand closed over the one above, and he hung, swinging wildly. He brought his left hand up, gave himself a few twisting heaves, and then he was sitting safely on the branch, panting like an exhausted runner.

He got up at last and climbed on up the trunk that was tapering now. He climbed fast and impatiently as though he were being pursued by someone, and at last he came to the very top.

He stood spell-bound, with the tiny green world stretched beneath, like a view from a picture book. The cows and the sheep in the far-off fields looked like tiny plasticine toys. A small cold breeze probed through his jersey making him shiver and the tree swayed gently, sending a quaint thrill through his stomach. Below him, down the great spine of fir, the pale brown branches jutted out like a framework of bones.

Neilly shouted, calling the names of the boys below, and soon he saw them, running like little gnomes over the field, and down the hill. He had to laugh at them. He could hear their thin excited chatter, as they pointed upwards, shading their eyes. Neilly hung there enraptured. His heart swelled and the keen fresh air stung the inside of his nostrils, making his eyes swim. Then at last he gave the boys one last wave and started down again. The boys still stood below pointing upwards engrossed in his descent.

When he reached the bare part again he sat on a branch, and swung his legs. He felt very calm, as though he were only stopping for a rest. Then gradually he became uneasy. He stood, rubbing his wrist over his lips, and glancing this way and that. Far, far below, so far that he now shuddered, he could see the boys still hunched together, pointing. He could hear their shouts, tiny pin points of sound. 'Ah he's stuck now. He'll never get down now ...'

Neilly circled the tree, searching for a toe hold, but the only one had vanished, when that dead branch had snapped beneath him. Hardly knowing what he was doing, he swung out on a branch and hung down weaving to and fro. He looked down along his chest beyond his twisting legs, feasting his eyes on the branches below. His feet clawed out, trying to grasp at them. Suddenly there was a crack and the branch broke! He gave a terrified cry, and his body dropped like a plummet.

With a shock that jarred his whole body, both his feet struck a branch directly underneath. He sagged forward, but at the same moment, his out-thrust hands closed over another branch above him, blocking his headlong fall. He hung for a moment, stretched between the two branches, in a kind of daze.

Then in a little while he recovered, and began to clamber on down. Once he missed his foothold, and almost fell again. He felt a streak of pain along the inside of his leg, above the knee, as a ragged twig tore the skin. But he continued on his way.

Gradually his strength and courage returned, and when he at last dropped back on to solid earth, he was smiling, and his eyes shone. The instant he hit the ground again, the boys swarmed around, cheering and clapping him on the back. Neilly retreated a few steps breathlessly.

'Good man, Neilly!' the boy in the red jersey was shouting. 'You did what nobody else here the day would have done. Boy-oh-boy when we seen you dropping down that bare part there, we sure thought you were a goner. Didn't we boys?'

'We sure did!' the rest of the boys chorused. 'That was powerful, Neilly.'

'Dropping down?' Neilly thought. 'Dropping down?' He opened his mouth to say, 'but the branch broke. I didn't drop. I fell!'

Then he stopped. If they thought he had dropped it, well, let them. He *would* have dropped it anyway, if the branch he was standing on hadn't broken off first and foremost. Of course he would! He would have dropped it like anything!

Anyway, fall, or drop, he had climbed the tree, and that's what nobody else had done. Ha, he'd shown them, so he had! They wouldn't jeer at him now! It wouldn't be 'poor wee Neilly' any more now ...

The boys brought his boots over for him, and the boy in the red jersey cleaned his muddy one with grass.

As Neilly was sitting down putting on his boots, his trousers slipped up, and he was surprised to see a long red scratch on his leg. Then he remembered where he had slipped on his downward journey.

The boys all bent down to examine the wound, and then they began advising him to come home, and get some iodine on it. Neilly smiled. It was only a scratch really, and not painful at all, but for some reason he felt terribly proud of it.

As the boys escorted him over the fields, home, he put on a slight limp, and every twenty yards or so, he would glance back at the middle fir that he'd climbed, and then down at his leg again, and then back to the fir again, and his eyes were shining with wonder and joy.

Old Clothes – Old Glory

Francis MacManus

*H*e came upon me before I had time, really, to re-
cognise him and to make plans for escape, the
mean plans that one makes in such circumstances. I
was loitering on the quays above O'Connell Bridge
in front of a second-hand bookshop, and so I
couldn't decently plead that I was in a hurry. I
know I was ashamed afterwards of the thought,
especially when I looked on his sunken cheeks,
stubbled black, and the cold eyes that had a queer
light in them, all like the emaciated face of a holy
man in a dark, smouldering Spanish painting. Also
as we spoke, I remembered the few scraps of his
story.

He shook my hand vaguely, and while I tried to
place him, he said, pointing to his hat and smiling
gravely: 'Look. That's Micky Cragan of Cork's hat.
And this is Petey Powell's overcoat, Petey Powell
of Limerick. He played a horse of a game last year,
didn't he? And this is Marty Lanigan's suit. He's a
terribly good-natured chap. Look it, I had only to
walk into his house and he ga' me it, and his
mother ga' me dinner. And look at the shoes.
They're like feathers on me feet. Jim Brett's. He
trains the lads. And me tie, that's a dandy. Jimmy
Crosse of Tipp ga' me that. I'm dressed for the

match, amn't I?'

The odd light was in his eye as he belted up the bulky over coat. Then I recognised him.

It wasn't the list of names that defined him in my memory, names of hurlers who had made throats go hoarse for cheering at finals in Croke Park, All-Ireland hurlers who were marked off for glory. It was the swaggering hitch of his shoulders that fixed him for me. I remembered Matty O'Meara.

'How are you Matty?'

He ignored the courtesy.

'Will the lads carry it off on Sunday?' he asked.

'Sunday?'

'The All-Ireland. I'm up for it.'

'So soon, Matty?'

That was on a Friday. It would be like him to be there, days before.

'I walked,' he added.

WHEN I WAS a growing lad, Matty O'Meara seemed to be a full-grown man. Of course he wasn't anything of the sort, but a young, lean, wiry fellow who, like his father and his brothers, a good family all, did a bit of gardening in our town. Matty's gardening was harmless, as my mother knew.

No sooner would he be out of sight of the house and the grown-ups, than he'd draw out a hurley from a ridge of potatoes or a heap of stones, slide his hands along it to finger the grain, and then begin to drive at the air. The odd light used to settle into his eyes then. The whole mind of the man, the power and control of his limbs, were focused on the balancing and swinging of that hurley.

'How's that, lads?' he'd shout to an unseen audience.

He'd pick up a pebble or a frostbitten potato and play at lobbing and pucking as if he had a real ball. Long graceful drives he had, and after every swing he'd stand still in a pose, his bare muscular arms crooked towards his left shoulder and the hurley curved around behind his head.

'How's that, lads? Matty O'Meara of Toomeveara won't be in it with me.'

From morning till night he'd practice like that, as long as nobody urged him to take the spade to the garden. There were a few other men like Matty in the town, men from whom he took his pattern. There was one in particular who for years and years as a paper-boy practised both hands with tiny pebbles for handball, pebbles that demanded exquisite precision to be struck at all by the palm of the hand or to be slung by crooked fingers. He became champion of Ireland. Matty, too, was shaping to be a champion, successor to the man of whom he was a namesake, for Matty O'Meara of Toomeveara was one of the most renowned goal-keepers of a long generation.

Our Matty would be a second and greater champion.

In those days, the town spawned little local hurling clubs. These were the breeding ground of a number of fine hurlers who earned their place at Croke Park in many a final. Matty wasn't a member of any particular club, but he hung around them all, playing with this team and that, now out on the field where he was a failure, now in the goal where he wasn't too bad. Then, one Sunday he played a miraculous game in goal, and some selectors were impressed, for Matty was told he'd get his chance of being tried out for the County team.

He walked the town in the evenings with a more rakish slant on his cap, a new swagger on his shoulders and a brighter glow in his cold eyes. He walked the streets with his hurley in hand, the symbol and instrument of his craft and profession.

'Matty O'Meara of Toomeveara!' someone would call out.

'How's that, lads?' he'd respond, and shifting his hurley deftly, he'd hold it up as if he were stopping and deadening a high ball. 'Wait till Sunday, lads. Wait till Sunday.'

It was the first, and I think the last time I heard him laughing.

He trained for that Sunday as no man ever trained before. He didn't do any gardening, although there was plenty to be done. It wasn't that he could afford to miss a day's work. No. But a champion was in the making, a champion was about to be tested, and the name of the O'Meara of Toomaveara would fade like an old moon. What was earning a living compared to that ? Or eating and drinking and going to bed of nights?

Matty stood against the gable-end of a house on which a goal had been marked with chalk, while other lads and myself pelted him with hurling balls from every angle. He was to stop them as they poured in.

I've seen some good goal-keepers, men whose calculated movement, whose swift action following close on swift but careful thought, was a delight, something to remember like music or fine dancing, or a piece of good verse. Rhythm, speed, coolness, all blended perfectly.

With his back to the gable-end, Matty was the incarnation of greatness. Remember, we could pelt balls, usually old and sodden, with force and accuracy, and we could direct them as we pleased; and sometimes we'd feint, making a deceptive swing of our arms, and then suddenly let go. I don't care. I don't care, but Matty leaped, sprang, slid and cast himself down, and somehow the blade of the hurley would snake out, meet the ball and stop it dead with a most satisfactory smack. Every angle, almost every ball! He would continue at that while our shoulders ached, and his eyes would burn and he would cheer himself.

He turned out to play before the selectors on that Sunday, and his togs were immaculate, his new cap was jaunty, and as he trailed his hurley, yellow with linseed oil, at his heels, a crowd of children followed him. He swaggered down to his goal, waved his hand to the crowd at the posts, who cried: 'Come on, Matty. The hard Matty O'Meara of Toomeveara', and not a man of them could have guessed that every word they uttered would be fuel for the vision's frenzy.

'Not a blade of grass will I let through,' he cried, 'not a breath.'

But then he did. He saved the first ball that sailed in hard, saved it in a free goal mouth and drove it comfortably up the field. Then, a ball dropped out of the sky and he caught it among a ruck of struggling men, twisted and wriggled for space, swung and cleared again. It was grand. He stood in a pose. The crowd howled and whooped. His eyes were like a cat's in the dark.'How's that, lads?'

'You'll be in Croke Park, Matty.'

'Come on, Stonewall O'Meara.'

And so he was ruined by whatever vision shook before his eyes and blinded him, for, after that, balls that a schoolboy could have stopped dribbled past him while he fumbled and staggered.

When the match was over, he sat down alone in the ditch, far apart from the rest. He was pale as dried clay. Nobody spoke to him, nobody offered a word to ease that pain which wrinkled his forehead and beaded his skin with perspiration, nobody except the young lads.

'Come on and dress yourself, Matty.'

'Don't take it so hard. It's nothing.'

He looked up dully, swaying his head.

'You'll do it yet, Matty.'

'O'Meara of Toomeveara.'

'Them was two great saves.'

Vision came back to his eyes as he said: 'Warn't they, though, warn't they? I'll do it yet. It's nothing. Them was great saves. I'll do it yet.'

THEN, WEEKS LATER, we heard that they had taken him away and locked him up in the asylum. We were told that his father and brothers could get no good of him and that he had begun to rise early on the mornings, almost with the first spark of the day, to go out into the fields behind the house with a hurley. That wasn't the worst of it. He could not be spoken to or checked. He would threaten with the hurley.

One night when it was just dark, he rose from his stool in his father's kitchen where he had been sitting silent, went down to a lower room and presently reappeared dressed in his hurling togs and with his stick in his hand.

'Where are you going at this hour of the night, son, in the name of God?'

'Keep back. The match. The match. I'll do it this time.'

They followed him out and discerned him in the dark, I suppose, by the white gleaming of the shorts that he had always kept spotless. He walked into the field behind the house and began to shout, to fill the night with cries, so that neighbours came to their doors and windows while men gathered out with bicycle lamps and lanterns.

'O'Meara of Toomeveara,' he shouted. 'Not a breath I'll let in. Here's the stone-wall. Hoo! Hoo! Hurroo!'

They crept up to him. He didn't notice them or the lamps that lit up the grass. He was crouching out in the dark like a man tensed in a goal who faces a whirl of hurlers from which a ball may light out like a bullet. He was shouting, turning his head to answer, as though all behind him were people whose roars tore through his soul like supreme joy. Suddenly, he straightened up as a lamp glowed on his face, fingered his cap and sighed. Tears glistened on his cheeks.

They led him away easily.

THOSE WERE THE things I recalled as we stood on the Dublin quay, beside the bookshop.

'I walked,' said he, 'all that way.'

'That's a very long walk,' I said.

'I've been all over Ireland. All the hurlers know me. Matty O'Meara of Toomeveara. But it's cold in the nights when you're caught out, and I'll have to take care of myself. The lads might be needing me. Your poor mother was good to me, God rest her. Look what I have on me.' Once more he pointed to the hat, the overcoat, the suit, the tie and the light shoes, and reeled off the names of men who could shake thousands. 'I'm dressed, amn't I? In the clothes of the best of 'em.'

'Who has a better right, Matty?'

The grave smile transfigured the cadaverous jaws and his sad mouth. He held his hands together, the left below the right, and moved his arms as though he swung a hurley. Then, with the light warming his cold eyes, sharpening his face, he wheeled from me, saying: 'I'll see you in Croke Park on Sunday', and set off down the quays, his mind astray on some field. And I knew that of all of the thousands who would be packed in the Park for the All-Ireland Final, even of all the men on the field itself, he would be the one in whom the fire of the game would mount to a consuming frenzy as he stood in the clothes of the champions and became all of them at once, every one.

The Distorting Mirror

Francis MacManus

*E*very fine evening at a quarter to five punctually, and even on drizzly evenings when one would see the pair of umbrellas floating along sedately above the arched balustrade of John's Bridge, the two Miss Myers passed through the lodge gates of the Castle Walk. Their stroll, if it could be called a stroll, since they peppered steadily along the gravelled river path at a hungry hen's gait, would empty their lungs of schoolroom air, purify the blood and give them a nice appetite for tea. The stroll always took one hour. The lads that buttressed the corners on that side of Kilkenny used to tell the time by the passing of the two ladies, and if they missed sight of them going, they were sure to remark them returning through the gates, punctually at a quarter to six.

The Miss Myers were unthinkable as existing separately. They were merely a distinction with little or no difference. They had the same kind of rosy cheeks, the same sort of plain, strong, black shiny shoes, the same rather oldish fashion in long narrow skirts which they fingered daintily as they stepped across puddles, and the same cut of black velvet throat-bands.They lived together; kept house together; went to Mass together – the Children's

Mass at ten; and idle wits declared they had decided at the same second of their lives never to marry. Of course, they taught together. Indeed, one did not merely go to St Peter's National School, where there were three or four other teachers, but to Miss Myer, for it was the elder of the sisters who was Principal. As for the other, the inseparable prostrate shadow, she was the other, the other Miss Myer.

Well, then, there was one fine evening – they themselves tell about it with blushes and agitated hands, while the other Miss Myer slips in timid comments and chimes in on the last word of the principal – there was one fine evening when they passed through the lodge gates at the usual time, and forsaking the dusty town, walked in the kindly sunshine that warmed the ancient walls and the old, heavy-crowned riverside seats.

One must fix the story together from their fragmentary recounting of it – and from their glances and gestures and silences.

Below the mill there is an embankment, surmounted by hedge-shaded seats, and dividing the river walk into an upper and lower path. There the two ladies seated themselves, for one is easily overcome by the drowsy warm valley air. Behind and below them was the other part of the divided walk, while before them the river shook like fluttered gold leaf. Side by side they were, Miss Myer the Principal, and the other Miss Myer the shadow. Then they heard a shrill, angry little voice: 'You should be in the other Miss Myer's class you dunderhead'.

The cry came from behind them, and one may be sure their rosy faces flushed suddenly and they turned to peer circumspectly through the clipped hedge to the walk below. It was so startling, so unnerving beside the quiet river, one did not know quite what to do. They sat still.

Below them, a little girl was seated on a tree stump before a semi-circle of large stones, and in her hand she brandished a long switch. Her face was puckered and crimson while she uttered gibberish and paused to point at a stone with the switch and command: 'Now, you say that after me'.

One noticed when she stood up that she had tied an apron around her waist to represent a long skirt and that she wore a thick band of black cloth around her neck.

'I think, dear,' whispered the other Miss Myer, 'I do think, dear, we had better continue our walk.' The Principal, fascinated, shook her head.

The child seated herself again, laid the switch across her knees, patted her hair and tucked in imaginary wisps while, with a sharp, rather ferocious side-long glance at the stones, she said: 'I'm watching you, Tommy Byrne. I'll give you a bee in your bonnet in a second, you noisy little pig. Attention, children. Fold your arms, everyone. Everyone, I said.' Restless, she arose once more, and gazing with assumed wide-eyed vacancy, she began to pinch and pull the skin of her neck between forefinger and thumb, and to make the circle of black cloth revolve. Her tiny mouth was pursed up as if it held an astringent crushed berry.

With a sudden movement and a shriek that

made the other Miss Myer murmur 'Oh!' the child wheeled, pointed with the stick and spluttered, 'Come out at once and toe the line, Thomas Byrne.' She stamped her feet in a frenzy. 'Come out this moment.' The stone, apparently, was loath to approach the fury, and then the switch came into action till the dust was furrowed on the walk and the child's arm became weary and her face bloodless. 'Send,' she stormed, 'send for the other Miss Myer.' The other Miss Myer arrived almost immediately. 'Take this brat,' said the child with a flounce, 'for he's only fit for the dunderheads.' Instantly, doubling her parts, the little girl changed over to the character of the other woman, saying in a whisper, with tiny bows and curtsies, 'Yes, Miss Myer. To be sure, Miss Myer. Come along now, Tommy, and be a good boy. Give me your hand. You'll promise to be a good boy, won't you'

'I'll take him Miss Myer.'

'Take him out of my sight and no petting,' said the child harshly.

There was quietness among the stones for a few moments, while the child passed jerkily up and down before the pupils and plucked at her neck. She was examining the classroom walls and muttering to herself.

The next act began with the same jerky suddenness. She leaped in alarm, put her hand in fear to her mouth, and said, 'Stand up, children. Mr Brand, the inspector.' The stones obeyed. She trotted forward, showing her teeth in an enforced smile, while her eyes were wide with fright, and panted, 'How are you, indeed, Mr Brand? We are delighted to see you. We did not expect you. No, Mr Brand. Yes, Mr Brand. Certainly, Mr Brand. To be sure, Mr Brand.' The switch was slipped to the ground, so that the little hands were free to flutter and pluck and entwine fingers. There was pleading in the stoop of the shoulders and the tilt of the head, and hysteria in the panted replies to the imaginary visitor. The child had become a fearful sycophant to the almost convincing ghost she had conjured out of the summer evening air.

One gathers that it was altogether horrible.

One surmises, too, that the ladies left the seat hurriedly, retraced their walk, and never regarded each other till, the Bridge regained, they could breathe freely. They looked at each other then. Now, there is nothing unusual in a lonely child playing school with sticks and stones, nor in a child caricaturing their teachers in the distorting mirror of her fancy – the two Miss Myers are too experienced with children to deny that – but one cannot be sure, when they regarded each other on the Bridge, that each did not behold a person who had been away, so to speak, in a foreign land for a long time and who had returned almost a stranger.

'It was completely unnerving,' says the elder Miss Myer, fingering her throat-band.

'Yes, unnerving,' chimes in the other Miss Myer.

And in the instant of recognition they glimpsed something of what they had become, of what had happened to their lives, unknown to themselves.

Last Bus for Christmas

Patricia Lynch

'*H*urry up there Miheal! Will ye bring over two red candles quick!'

'More strawberry jam, Miheal! Two one pound jars! And raisins: four one-pound bags!'

'Miheal Daly! I'm wore out wid waitin' for twine. How can I parcel the customers' groceries wid ne'er an inch of string?'

Miheal grabbed a handful of string from the box in the corner behind the biscuit tins and ran with it to Mr Coughlan. He brought the jam and the raisins at the same time to Peter Cadogan, and rolled the candles along the counter to Jim Rearden. then he went back to his job of filling half-pound bags with sugar.

Miheal was the shopboy and, one day, if he worked hard and behaved himself, Mr Coughlan had promised to make him an assistant.

'There's grandeur for an orphan!' Mrs Coughlan told him. 'You should be grateful.'

Miheal was grateful. But as he watched the women crowding the other side of the counter, filling market bags and baskets with Christmas shopping, he was discontented. Yet he had whistled and sung as he put up the coloured paper chains and decorated the windows with yards of tinsel and artificial holly.

He nibbled a raisin and gazed out at the sleet drifting past the open door.

Everybody's going home for Christmas but me, he thought.

The Coughlans always went to their relations for Christmas. Mrs Coughlan always left Miheal plenty to eat and Mr Coughlan gave Miheal a shilling to spend. But Miheal never ate his Christmas dinner until they came back. After Mass he spent Christmas Day walking about the streets, listening to the noise and the clatter that came from the houses.

'Only two more hours,' whispered Peter Cadogan, as Miheal brought him bags of biscuits and half-pounds of rashers as fast as Mr Coughlan could cut them.

'Two more sugars, Miheal,' said Jim Rearden. 'Where d'you get your bus?'

Jim was new. He didn't know Miheal was an orphan, and Miheal was ashamed to tell him he had no home to go to for Christmas.

'Ashton's Quay,' he muttered.

'We'll go together,' said Jim over his shoulder. 'I've me bag under the counter. Get yours!'

The next time Miheal brought Jim candles and raisins the new assistant wanted to know what time Miheal's bus went.

'I'll just make it if I run,' said Miheal.

'Then get your bag, lad. Get your bag!'

Miheal slipped through the door leading to the house. He ran to his little dark room under the stairs. He didn't dare switch on the light. Mrs

Coughlan would want to know what he was doing. And a nice fool he'd look if she found out he was pretending to go home for Christmas.

'Home!' said Miheal to himself. 'That's where a lad's people come from and mine came from Carrigasheen.'

He wrapped his few belongings in a water-proof. He grabbed his overcoat from the hook behind the door and was back in the shop before Mr Coughlan could miss him.

'Hi, Miheal! Give me a hand with this side of bacon. I never cut so many rashers in me life!'

Miheal pushed his bundle under the counter and ran to help.

'Isn't it grand to be going home for Christmas!' cried Peter, as they closed the door to prevent any more customers from coming in.

'Isn't it terrible to be turning money away!' groaned Mr Coughlan.

But Mrs Coughlan was waiting for him in her best hat and the coat with the fur collar.

'Can I trust you lads to bolt the shop door an' let yourselves out the side door?' demanded Mr Coughlan.

'Indeed you can, sir!' replied Peter and Jim.

The last customer was served.

'I'm off!' cried Peter.

'Safe home!' called the others.

Then Jim was running down the quay, Miheal stumbling after him, clasping his bundle, his un-buttoned coat flapping in the wind.

They went along Burgh Quay, pushing by the people waiting for the Bray bus, then down to

Ashton's Quay.

'There's me bus!' shouted Jim.

"Tis packed full!' murmured Miheal. He was terribly sorry for Jim. But maybe he would come back with him and they could spend Christmas together.

The bus was moving.

Jim gave a leap, the conductor caught his arm and pulled him to safety. He turned and waved to Miheal, his round red face laughing. He would have to stand all the way but Jim was used to standing.

Two queues still waited. Miheal joined the longest.

'Where are ye bound for, avic?' asked a stout countrywoman, with a thin little girl and four large bundles, who came up after him.

'Carrigasheen!' replied Miheal proudly.

'Ah well! I never heard tell of the place. But no doubt ye'll be welcome when ye get there. An' here's the bus.'

'I'll help with the bundles, ma'am,' said Miheal politely.

Now every seat was filled. Still more people squeezed into the bus. Miheal reached the step.

'One more an' one more only!' announced the conductor.

'In ye go ma'am!' said Miheal, stepping back.

The little girl was in. Miheal pushed the bundles after her and everyone cried out when the conductor tried to keep back the stout woman.

'Sure ye can't take the child away from her mammy!' declared a thin man. 'Haven't ye any

Christianity in your bones?'

'Can't she sit on me lap?' demanded the stout woman. 'Give me a h'ist up, lad. And God reward ye!' she added, turning to Miheal.

He seized her under the arms. She caught the shining rail and Miheal gave a great heave.

He stood gazing after the bus.

'Now I'm stranded!' he said, forgetting he had no need to leave Dublin.

A dash of sleet in Miheal's face reminded him. He could go back to the lonely house behind the shop. His supper would be waiting on the table in the kitchen. He could poke up the fire and read his library book.

The quays were deserted. A tall garda strolled along. He stared curiously at Miheal and his bundle.

'Missed the bus, lad?' he asked.

"Twas full up,' explained Miheal.

'Bad luck!' sympathised the garda. 'Can ye go back where ye came from?'

Miheal nodded.

"Tis a bad night to be travelling!' said the garda. 'That's the way to look at it.'

He gave Miheal a friendly nod and passed on.

I'd as well be getting me supper, thought Miheal.

But he did not move.

Over the Metal Bridge came a queer old coach drawn by two horses. The driver was wrapped in a huge coat with many capes and a broad-rimmed hat was pulled down over his twinkling eyes.

He flourished a whip and pulled up beside

Miheal.

The boy edged away. He didn't like the look of the coach at all.

The driver leaned over and managed to open the door at the side with his whip.

'In ye get! Last bus for Christmas!'

Whoever saw a bus with horses! thought Mihaul. But I suppose they use any old traps at Christmas.

Still he held back.

'All the way to Carrigasheen widout stoppin'!' said the driver.

Miheal could see the cushioned seats and the floor spread thick with fresh hay. The wind, which was growing fiercer and colder every moment, blew in his face. He gave one look along the desolate quay and, putting his foot on the iron step, scrambled in.

At once the door slammed shut. The driver gave a shout and the horses trotted over the stones.

The coach bumped and swayed. Miheal tried to stretch out on the seat, but he slipped to the floor. The hay was thick and clean. He put his bundle under his head for a pillow and fell asleep.

An extra bump woke him up.

'I never thought to ask the fare,' said Miheal to himself. 'Seems a long way, so it does. Would he want ten shillings? He might – easy! Well, I haven't ten shillings. I've two new half-crowns. He'll get one and not a penny more!'

He tried to stand up, but the coach was swaying from side to side and he had to sit down again.

'Mister! Mister!' he shouted. 'How much is the

fare?'

The rattle of the coach and the thunder of the horses' hooves made so much noise he could scarcely hear himself. Yet he could not keep quiet.

'I won't pay more than two and six,' he shouted. 'Mind now! I'm telling you.'

The door of the coach swung open and Miheal was pitched out, his bundle following him. He landed on a bank covered with snow and lay there blinking.

The road wound away through the mountains in the moonlight – an empty desolate road. The wind had dropped but snow was falling.

In the distance he could hear a strange sound. It was coming nearer and nearer, and soon Miheal knew it was someone singing *Adeste Fidelis* in a queer cracked voice.

The singer approached, tramping slowly along: an old man with a heavy sack on his back.

'What ails ye to be sitting there in the snow, at this late hour of the night, young lad?' he asked, letting his sack slip to the ground.

'I came on the coach from Dublin,' replied Miheal, standing up.

He was ashamed to say he had fallen out.

The old man pushed back his battered caubeen and scratched his head.

'But there hasn't been a coach on this road in mortal memory!' he declared. 'There's the bus road the other side of the mountain and the last bus went by nigh on two hours ago. I suppose ye came by that. Where are you bound for?'

'Mebbe I did come by the bus and mebbe I

didn't!' exclaimed Miheal. 'But I'd be thankful if you'd tell me am I right for Carrigasheen?'

The old man wasn't a bit annoyed by Miheal's crossness.

'D'ye see the clump of trees where the road bends round by the mountain? There's Carriga-sheen! I'm on me way there an' I'll be real glad of company. So ye're home for Christmas? I thought I knew everyone for miles around, yet I don't re-member yer face. What name is on ye, lad?'

'Miheal Daly.'

'There are no Dalys in Carrigasheen now. That I do know! But we can talk as we go. Me own name is Paudeen Caffrey.'

Miheal caught up the sack. He was a strong lad but he found it heavy. He wondered how the old man had managed to carry it all. Paudeen Caffrey took the boy's bundle and they set off. The snow piled on their shoulders, on the loads they carried, on their hair, their eyebrows, but they did not notice, for Miheal was telling the old man all about himself.

'So me poor gossoon, ye're an orphan?' asked the old man.

'I am indeed!' agreed Miheal.

'An' ye haven't a father or mother, or brother or sister to be friend to ye?'

'Not a soul!'

'An' these people ye work for, what class of people are they?' continued old Paudeen Caffrey.

'Not too bad!' declared Miheal. 'Aren't they going to make me an assistant one of these days?'

'Suppose now,' began the old man. 'Mind, I'm

just saying suppose – ye have a chance to be shop-boy to an old man and his wife that needed help bad in their shop and couldn't get it? Mind ye – I'm only supposing. Ye'd have a room wid two windas, one lookin' out on the market square, the other at the mountains. Ye'd have three good meals a day, a snack at supper, ten shillings a week, an' if you wanted to keep a dog or a cat, or a bicycle, ye'd be welcome. What would ye say to that?'

He looked at Miheal sideways and Miheal looked back.

'It wouldn't be with Paudeen Caffrey, that kept the corner shop next to the post office, would it?' asked Miheal.

'It would so,' replied the old man.

'I'm remembering now,' said the boy. 'Me father told me if ever I needed a friend to write to Paudeen Caffrey.'

'Why didn't ye, lad? Why didn't ye?'

'I was ashamed. My mother told me how they left Carrigasheen after telling everyone they were going to Dublin to make their fortunes an', when they came back, they'd be riding in their carriage. Ye see?'

The old man laughed.

'An' didn't ye come back in a carriage? But there's the lights of Carrigasheen. Do ye want to come home wid me, Miheal Daly?'

'If you'll have me, Mr Caffrey.'

The old man chuckled.

'An to think I went out for a sack of praties an' come back wid a shop boy! Wasn't it well ye caught the last bus for Christmas, Miheal?'

'It was indeed!' declared Miheal Daly.

He could see the corner shop with the door open and an old woman looking out. Beyond her he caught a glimpse of firelight dancing on the walls, of holy pictures framed in holly and a big red Christmas candle on the table waiting for the youngest in the house to light it.

Acknowledgements

The author and publisher would like to thank the following authors, publishers and copyright holders for their permission to use stories for which they hold the copyright.

The Roberta Kanal Theatrical Agency and Felicity Hayes McCoy for 'The Giant's Wife'; C. J. Fallon, Dublin for 'Cliona's Wave' by Sinead de Valera; 'The Ghost of the Valley' reproduced with permission of Curtis Brown Ltd, London: copyright the trustees of the estate of Lord Dunsany; Mrs D. L. Martin for 'Godfather Death' by Gerard Murphy; Patrick MacManus for 'Old Clothes – Old Glory' and 'The Distorting Mirror' by Francis MacManus; Eugene and Mai Lambert for 'Last Bus for Christmas' by Patricia Lynch; and Mercier Press for 'The Ant' and 'The Fox and the Hedgehog' by Michael Scott, 'The Four Magpies' and 'The Trapper' by Sigerson Clifford and 'The Boy who had no Story' by Kevin Danaher.

MORE MERCIER BESTSELLERS

IRISH ANIMAL TALES
Michael Scott

'Have you ever noticed how cats and dogs sometimes sit up and look at something that is not there?
Have you ever seen a dog barking at nothing? And
have you ever wondered why? Perhaps it is because
the animals can see the fairy folk coming and going
all the time, while humans can only see the Little
People at certain times ...'

ENCHANTED IRISH TALES
Patricia Lynch

Enchanted Irish Tales tells of ancient heroes and
heroines, fantastic deeds of bravery, magical king-
doms, weird and wonderful animals ... This new
illustrated edition of classical folktales, retold by
Patricia Lynch with all the imagination and warmth
for which she is renowned, rekindles the age-old
legends of Ireland, as exciting today as they were
when first told.

THE CHILDREN'S BOOK OF IRISH FOLKTALES
Kevin Danaher

These tales are filled with the mystery and adventure of a land of lonely country roads and isolated
farms, humble cottages and lordly castles, rolling
fields and tractless bogs. They tell of giants and
ghosts, of queer happenings and wondrous deeds, of
fairies and witches and of fools and kings.